BTWN

A NOVEL ABOUT IDENTITY

LAKE

AND THE GREATER UNIVERSE WITHIN

&SEA

Jalal Moughania

THE MAINSTAY
FOUNDATION

Author: Jalal Moughania

© 2018 The Mainstay Foundation

Printed in the United States.

ISBN: 978-1943393435

Dedication

To the man who taught us that we are not insignificant, that rather within each of us lies the greater universe…

CONTENTS

1. THE ICU

I was lost. I couldn't find my way around this hospital if my life depended on it. So I looked for someone to ask in the area I found myself in having read a sign titled "Cardiovascular Unit". Not sure how close I was to where I needed to be, I had already passed by the hospital's main Help Desk about fifteen minutes ago and there was no turning back now. To my luck I finally found someone.

"Excuse me. I'm trying to find the ICU. Could you point me in the right direction?" I interrupted the nurse across the hallway, as she was charting what I assumed to be some pretty important medical information on her clipboard. My question inadvertently caused her to jerk her neck back and stop her in her tracks. I could see her eyes now. Moments ago they were veiled by her eyelids as she looked down at that plain brown clipboard. A deep blue ocean unraveled as she looked up at me to address a question that she probably received all the time. But she was deep in thought and the depth of her eyes coincided pretty well. The way she pressed her eyebrows together made her look serious, but still kind. Almost concerned, she opens her mouth to answer my question.

"Oh you're pretty far from here sweetheart. But it's okay, believe it or not I still get lost around here. Take the elevators around the corner up to the fourth floor. Make a right. Walk down until you see a water fountain. Take a left and walk down a long hallway until you see the ICU sign."

I nodded my head as if I had understood the nurse's directions. But for the life of me I couldn't fathom a word she said. It was as if my brain had been thrown in that deep blue ocean that I saw in her eyes. I could not process the words I heard because my mind was too busy thinking about swimming. As a kid who spent a few years of his childhood in Lebanon, I swam on the shores of the Mediterranean Sea. Oh, What I would do to be back there right now.

"You got it?"

I need to stop swimming.

"Yes, thank you very much," I replied and hurried along.

Somehow her words managed to get lobbed in my subconscious. I was able to finally end up at that long hallway that ended with the plain ICU sign hanging right above two doors that opened up in opposite directions as nurses and doctors walked through them.

As I walked down that long narrow hallway towards the intensive care unit, it felt like the longer I walked the farther the doors became. The walls were a deafening white, so bare that any blemish could be seen with just a moment of reflection. A part of me thought about turning back. Does she even want to see me? What would she say? What would I say? I hadn't seen my mother in over a year. And now she was in the hospital being treated for something I neither could pronounce or understand. When I finally reached the double door entry, something compelled me to pause for a moment. I slowly raised my head up and looked up to the sky, well to the ceiling, and said a prayer.

God, forgive our sins and the sins of our parents.
Have mercy on them just as they had mercy on us as
children. Reward their good deeds with your generosity,
and forgive their misdeeds with your grace.
Amen.

That's a prayer my father taught me as a child. I would hear him supplicate that in his deep, slow, methodical voice during the *qunoot* of his daily prayer. I realized at that same moment, after sending that prayer to the Heavens, that I hadn't prayed in months. And by pray I don't mean the five daily prayers of a practicing Muslim. I hadn't prayed, asked for, supplicated, or spoken to God in about 13 weeks.

How proud would my mother be to see me now? I took my chances and walked through those doors to see her. I looked at my phone to remember what room number she was in.

"Mama is in Room 414. See you soon Ali. Love you." I reread the message from my sister Emily – the favorite child of my parents and rightfully so. They would never say this but Emily is really their pride and joy. Straight-A student with an impeccable reputation in and outside of school. Valedictorian of her class, she went on to receive a scholarship at the University of Michigan.

She graduated with her bachelor's degree at the age of 19 and went on to law school, also on a scholarship. Emily was slender, fair skinned, modest in every meaning of the word, and yet so beautiful. This is all the while her "older" brother struggled with indecisiveness throughout high school and reluctantly went to college only to graduate five years later with a degree in history. I do love history though.

My thoughts are racing and I do not know what to expect. Well I do but I cannot settle myself into the reality that is before me. My mother is ill and I haven't had the decency to check up on her until she was brought into this godforsaken place. I hate hospitals. "Become a doctor," people said as I grew up. Why? So I can watch people die and be reminded of how miserable life can be when you're all alone? But my mother wasn't alone. Even if I wasn't there, she had people that waited to see her, to talk to her, to benefit from her grace. You see, Emily takes after my mother – a person filled with hope and faith. It's funny because when people ask about how Emily was named they're usually taken aback by the creativity involved in her namesake.

My family is a mix of Iraqi and Lebanese culture. My father is Iraqi and my mother is Lebanese. And they both come from conservative towns from their home countries. Naturally, they would be inclined to give their children traditional Arabic names given their mother tongue and their much adored culture. My mom was always the creative one. In naming her kids, she said, "Why can't they have the best of both worlds?"

My father was always amused and impressed by my mother's creativity.

"And what would that be *azizati*?" My dear.

"This one is my hope."

"So you want to name her *Emal* – Hope."

"My hope. Add a 'y' to that. Emal-y. And she's American. So she'll be *Emily*."

My father would smile and nod his head. He embraced my mother and said, "I love it."

And there she was, the little Muslim girl named Emily not with the intent to be "Americanized" but merely as a product of her mother's belief that you can be who you are, with all the richness of your homeland's heritage, and be an American too. "You don't need to sacrifice one for the other," she would tell us growing up. I didn't believe her. I still don't. Even if my sister's name is Emily, she still couldn't walk through certain neighborhoods without me by her side. Though I wasn't the most focused or studious student, I definitely wasn't a kid you wanted to mess with. Being over six feet tall and about 210 pounds of muscle was a plus in high school. It still is today, even though I haven't been to the gym in a while so I'm lacking on the muscle aspect.

As I walked closer to my mom's hospital room I saw my cousin standing outside the room with one foot against the wall behind him as the other propped him up at a slant. It was Adam. He was only a couple years older than me but I always looked up to him like an uncle. He was the coolest guy you would know and was always there for everybody, family and friends alike. So it wasn't a surprise to see him there.

"What's up cousin?" I said as I got near. His hands were in his pocket, eyes glued to the ground. He lifted his head up, as I disrupted his staring contest with the floor.

"Hey, bud. How's it going?"

He wasn't his normal self. He was distraught, nervous, and seemed like he hadn't slept in days. For the guy that was most of the family's pillar to lean on, seeing him like this wasn't a good sign.

"How's mom doing?" I asked knowing that I should just go in there to see for myself. I couldn't shake off my indecisiveness and hesitation.

"She's been asking about you Ali. She misses you." He gestured with his head to go in there and see her.

I mustered the courage to walk into her room only to find her praying. Because if she wasn't teaching, cooking, laughing, or reciting, she was praying. Because that's the kind of person she is. My sister Emily was inside with her back to the door preparing some food for my mom so that she could eat something as soon as she was done. I sat down on a wooden foldable chair near the door. My sister saw me as she turned around. She smiled slightly and walked across the room to embrace me. For a five-foot-two, petite girl, she really had a tight grip. Emily looked up at me with her round green eyes and whispered,

"Where've you been? We miss you."

How do I explain that I've been so close yet so far? That I could have come sooner but I simply didn't. That I want to see them every day but just can't get myself to do it.

"I'm here now aren't I?" I said with a half broken smile.

"Yes. Yes, you are," Emily whispered and smiled ear-to-ear. That smile could light up a warehouse let alone a hospital room. Things were so much brighter with Emily around. I missed her a lot.

"She's not doing so well Ali."

"What's wrong? What are the doctors saying?"

Emily hesitated. She looked back at mom, who seemed like she was finishing up her prayers.

"Maybe we should step outside and talk about it." Emily began walking me out of the room.

"Is that Habibi Ali?" My beloved Ali. That's what she always called me. I turned back to see my mom adjusting herself as she tried to sit upright in her hospital bed. IV lines crisscrossed across her body. Screens around her monitored her vitals. Her body looked frail but her heart wouldn't waiver. I could feel her strength, but it was withering hour by hour.

"Habibi ya Ali, come here." She extended her arms out to me like she used to when I was a child. No matter how bad I was she always had her arms out open to me. No matter what I could have done to disappoint her, her love was always unconditional. I could always turn to her. It was completely my choice when I did not. A choice that I made time to time and would regret so deeply after realizing my loss.

"Salaam mama. How are you?" I said as I walked slowly toward her bedside. The closer I got the more I saw how tired she looked. She was much thinner even though she had always been slender. Her veins could be seen more apparently through her skin. Her lips were dry and darker shadows enveloped her eyes. It seemed as if she had aged 10 years in just a few months' time.

"I'm doing great alhamdulillah, how are you?" She never tried to make me feel guilty when she talked to me, but I always did. In fact, she intently spoke to me as if I had seen her on a daily basis. However, that only made me feel worse. Her kindness reminded me of my cruel neglect. Her compassion exposed my selfishness and lack of care. I think that was partially why I took so long to come see her. I was afraid of being reminded. I was afraid of being exposed.

"Hey son!" My dad's deep voice filled the room from behind me. I turned around finding him putting down about six different bags of food, sweets, and other miscellaneous things. That's how I remember him growing up. His hands were always full when he came home. Whether it was in our home or in the home of our family or friends, I never did see him empty handed. My father was a generous man to friends, family, and strangers alike. I would never forget a particular display of generosity for my dad that took place about twelve years ago.

When I was twelve years old we went on a family trip to Florida. Guess where? You got it. Disney World! Even for a high school football player, I was pretty geeked about this trip. I love Disney. I grew up watching Disney, it was practically part of my hardwire. Aladdin and The Lion King were my absolute favorite. So on the flight to Orlando our seats were all mixed up at check-in for some reason and none of us were sitting next to each other. Emily was in 11B, Mom was in 21A, Dad was in 14A and I was in 14C. There was this guy sitting between my dad and I for some reason. He didn't want to switch even when my dad offered him my aisle seat. Little did he know I wasn't giving up that aisle seat. Leg room nation!

So without even thirty minutes into the flight, my dad and the dude sitting between us hit it off. They were talking, laughing, and rubbing elbows like they've been friends for decades. At that point I was so relieved the guy didn't take my dad up on his offer for my seat, because if I had to be stuck in between those two in that laugh-match I think I would have passed out. Well, I still passed out regardless. I happen to be a very heavy and a very easy sleeper. I think I am one medical prerequisite away from being diagnosed with narcolepsy. Maybe not.

Before I knew it I was waking up to the flight attendant's announcement of landing. I didn't even wake up to the landing itself. Man, I was really knocked out cold.

"Ladies and gentlemen, on behalf of this airline's cabin crew we would like to welcome you to Orlando, Florida where the temperature is currently 83 degrees Fahrenheit."

We unfastened those lousy seatbelts and stretched out of the tiny seats. We were finally back on the ground and it felt great.

"It was a pleasure to meet you Jimmy."

"The pleasure was all mine *Hajj*." Yeah he called my dad "Hajj". Why? Because everyone called my dad Hajj. It was his nickname, not like how every person who goes to the pilgrimage in *Mecca* earns the title of Hajj but because he was called that since he was a kid. My dad went to the pilgrimage at the age of fourteen. Yes, sir. He actually paid for the trip himself and went to Hajj basically when he started high school. A true boss right there. So that's what he's been called for most of his life. Even my grandma has been calling him Hajj longer than she's called him Hussain.

Jimmy and my dad exchanged contact information and promised to stay in touch. As Jimmy was shaking my dad's hand farewell, the ring on my dad's right hand caught his eye. "That's a beautiful ring Hajj. I've never seen anything like it."

Jimmy was Italian. Naturally my dad took a liking to him because of the Mediterranean connection. Even though my dad was Iraqi, he spent much of his life in Syria and Lebanon – both on the Mediterranean – because of the persecution he and his family faced under Saddam Hussein during the Baathist rule in Iraq. He doesn't talk about it much but whenever he does, he always tears up. Mom always used to tell us it would be hard for us to understand the pain that he went through given that we grew up here in America.

"Oh this here… this is called *Durr Najaf*. It was a gift from a dear friend of mine years ago before I left Iraq. It's a sacred stone…" This particular Durr Najaf is similar to what we would call a white opal, hand carved from the mountains of northern Iraq and placed atop a silver band with the engraving that read in Arabic, "There is enough light for those who wish to see..." eternal words by my father's idol *Imam Ali*. The ring also happened to be a gift from a scholar my father was dear friends with growing up in Iraq. He gave it to my father before he left the country in the eighties.

"It sure is a beautiful ring. Do you know how I could get one of those?"

My dad smiled at Jimmy. When I saw that smile my jaw dropped. I knew what he was about to do and I just couldn't believe it.

"The ring is yours Jimmy." My dad took off his white stone ring, one that he had worn for years and almost never took off, and placed it in Jimmy's palm.

"Oh no! I couldn't do that. I can't possibly accept this Hajj," said Jimmy as he gazed further at the ring. Jimmy was a bad liar, but still a nice guy. Just a really bad liar. My dad could tell too, it made him chuckle a bit and smile wider.

"I insist. In my culture, when a friend or a stranger takes a liking to something that is ours, we offer it from our hearts. The only thing that this doesn't apply to is our women. But you're Italian so you should know what I mean."

They both burst into laughter and by that point the whole plane was laughing. The entire exchange was being watched by the rest of the passengers around us as we waited for the gate to clear for exit. It's funny that everyone was so at ease around him in that airplane. Even though he was a good looking guy, he still was a bearded Middle Easterner. It didn't seem to matter for my dad. His charm and kindness usually overshadowed people's shallow judgments. They were simply in awe.

Yup. That was my dad. A man people admired and were simply in awe of. I often wondered how I fell so far from the tree? The reminiscing quickly ended with my dad's deadly bear hug in that small hospital room.

My dad grabbed me so tight I felt like he was making up for all the hugs I hadn't given him in the past few months with that one embrace. It was pretty tight. "I can't breathe," I gasped.

"Good," he said and let me go. I dropped back down from the few inches he had lifted me up off the ground. He wasn't as subtle or gentle as my mom was. "Where've you been Ali?"

I looked at my dad and I couldn't give him an answer. I turned to my right and saw Emily look down at the empty screen on her phone as to try not to add to the tension that was surely ensuing. I looked toward my mom for some consolation. She gazed back at me trying to smile but seemed to be more worried about me even though she was the one in a hospital bed. The problem is I really didn't know.

I don't know where I've been. Things have been like a blur for me, especially lately.

"School and work," I managed to say to my dad even though it had been over a year since I graduated. I was just so used to giving that answer to whoever asked. In that hospital room, I was their 24-year-old son with a seemingly useless degree in history that gave me no real job prospects. I looked off through the window where we had a glamourous view of the parking lot. Did I mention that I hated that hospital, and really all hospitals for that matter? People coming and going in and out of the hospital to visit ill ones because of a sense of obligation they had. Were they really there because they wanted to be there? Probably not. That's not why I was visiting mom though. I actually wanted to be there, however, it didn't seem like that to dad because of how MIA I've been.

"Well, we miss you and we're happy you're here now." Mom smiled at me and gestured for me to come sit next to her on that comfy hospital bed. She flattened out the sheet with her small hands. The most beautiful hands the world has ever seen. With those hands she gave me everything. I was just too stupid, too naïve, too immature to realize it or appreciate it. If I did I would have spent the time that I had left kissing those hands and seeking God's grace through them. Instead, I said this...

"I gotta run. I'm working a night shift again at the station. I'll come back soon."

"I thought you were done working at Yasser's gas station Ali? What happened to that research position you said you secured at the university?" My dad questioned.

"I'm just helping cousin Yasser out until he finds someone reliable." I replied.

"And the research position?" He wouldn't let it go.

I hadn't secured a research position. I just said that in passing one night to my dad so he would stop worrying and ease up on me a bit. I honestly did apply for dozens of research jobs though, but none of them ever got back to me. It became so frustrating I pretty much gave up. Almost five years and thousands of dollars in loans spent on a history degree, for what? So I could keep putting in shifts at Yasser's gas station? But I couldn't say that to my dad. It would just be further disappointment.

"It's in the works dad. I'm still substitute teaching during the week too. We'll see what happens." I said with some hope.

My dad wasn't impressed. It was beating around the bush that disappointed him the most, but it was hard to give him a straight answer.

"That's great to hear habibi. Maybe you should spend more time teaching. Ever since you were a boy you loved to share and inspire others. If the research position isn't panning out, maybe teaching is really your calling. Everything happens for a reason..." Mom said with a cough.

I smiled. "Thank you mom."

A few seconds passed with just silence and I knew I couldn't stay any longer. I leaned in and gave my mom a pathetic peck on the cheek, my sister an apathetic pat on the shoulder and my dad an awkward hand shake. I don't know why I did this. I don't know why I do a lot of things. Sometimes I just don't know how to act.

I walked out of the hospital room and Adam was still there. Well it really was only a few minutes.

"Short visit, cousin?"

"Yeah I have to get going to work. I'll see you around."

I tried walking past him, but he grabbed me by the arm. He really did have a hard grip.

"You need to be here for her. She doesn't have much time left."

I looked at him and saw the pain in his eyes. The mix of emotions between my mom's situation and my lack of presence was getting to him. The hallway was empty. I looked around at the deafening white walls and could only think about how I had to get out of there. His grip got tighter.

"Are you hearing me Ali? Where are you bro?" He looked me straight in the eyes. That look pierced right through me. I couldn't reciprocate.

I pulled my arm away and got loose of his grip. I didn't say anything. I couldn't. I didn't have an answer for him and I couldn't really come up with something else because I choked. I darted towards the elevators and pressed the ground level.

I had to get out of there. I couldn't breathe.

2. THE PARTY

The sound of cars zooming by. The echoes of sirens faintly blaring in the distance. Still, it was way too close to hear it all vividly. I didn't live next to a highway or a major road. My street was never that busy, no matter how rowdy our neighborhood streets got. I started moving from my side as I awakened and immediately felt the pain shoot down from my shoulder to my thigh. It was as if I had slept on concrete. Turns out I kind of did.

"Where the hell am I?" I thought to myself.

Quickly realizing that I wasn't in my bedroom, or any bedroom for that matter, I looked around and had no idea where I was. I was overwhelmed and felt a panic attack coming. Yeah, I get those sometimes, yet no one knows. I tried to calm myself down.

"Relax. You're fine," I said to myself.

But I knew I wasn't fine. I knew this wasn't going to be okay nor was it 'okay' for me to end up where I was. I found myself on the sloping grassy hill that connects with the local park off of Hines Drive. I woke up in Hines Park. A storm of images rushed through my mind from what I could remember from last night, and then it hit me.

Jason, his friends, and I were here last night for a late night drive. We decided to stop by and hang out at the park during the late hours when no one else was around. Jason had called me up to go on that drive at about 10pm.

"Hey Al, what are you up to man?" Jason asked.

"Nothing much. Chillin' at home." I said as I was laying down on my comfy sofa in the basement browsing through Instagram pictures on my iPhone. It was my first night off in months. Between substitute teaching hormonal junior high kids and the extra night shifts I was pulling at Yasser's gas station, I was beat. So I took full advantage of it. My night off looked like this. Feet propped up on the edge of the couch with extra pillows. Netflix on the flat screen. A bowl of popcorn in my lap. A can of pop in my left hand and my iPhone in my right. Life was good.

"Come out for a ride with me. I'm meeting up with a few friends. We'll go find a place to chill at."

"I'm already chillin' here. How about you come by?" I replied lazily.

"Nah man. We'll have fun. I want you to meet some of my new friends too. Cool people. It'll be crispy. You'll like it," Jason assured me.

I paused. "I guess I could continue this when I come back," I thought to myself. "How far are you?" I asked him.

"I'm like five minutes away from your house. You ready?"

"Yeah. I'll be out in a few."

I knew Jason from undergrad, we had taken Ancient Greek History together and were probably the only two guys interested in the subject. He wasn't a nerd either, he was quite the jock like me but still appreciated his brain. He told me that he decided to turn down a football scholarship to focus on school and save whatever brain cells he still had left. I heard from some people that grew up with us that he didn't pass the drug exam for the program and that's why he didn't play. He was in and out with the wrong crowd. Who really knows, right?

Jason was a cool guy, always chill. Throughout undergrad we ate lunch together quite a bit and would often hit the gym between classes. He had a good attitude and knew how to have a good time without getting too stupid or too crazy. Yes, stupid and crazy can be different. Some of his friends though, I would find out, were both stupid and crazy. Not so chill.

Jason and I were in a separate car, driving in a grey Jeep Cherokee to meet his friends up at the park. As we pulled in, I watched one of the guys pull out a bottle of something from the backseat of his black Dodge Charger. Zayd I think his name was – they all called him Zee or maybe it was Zeek I'm not sure. I remember looking at his car, admiring how beautiful it was from the outside. That smooth metallic black exterior, dark limo tinted windows, double exhaust mufflers, xenon white fog lights, and of course the smoked custom twenty inch rims. What a beauty.

But as soon as he opened the backseat door to pull out that bottle, all that beauty went away. I despised him in that moment. But I would despise myself even more for what would follow.

Before I could even introduce myself to Jason's friend, the deafening music blasting from the Bose speakers of the Charger took precedence.

"We're going to party tonight!" Zeek shouted.

He danced around with that bottle in his hand like a drunkard monkey. One of the girls with him then popped open the trunk. Lo and behold! More drinks. There were two girls, I never really got their names, sitting in the back of his car and another friend, Abdul, that came out from the front. I knew Abdul from high school. I remember him as a quiet kid that kept mostly to himself. He was to himself most of that night too. Abdul would occasionally laugh at Zeek as he made a fool out of himself.

I looked at Jason and whispered, "Jay, you know I don't drink man."

It wasn't much of a whisper since I could barely hear myself think with Zeek's obnoxious music booming in the background.

"I stopped drinking too. We don't have to drink, Zeek is doing all the drinking for us," he laughed and gave me a light shove. Watching Zeek was kind of funny actually, but I tried not to laugh.

Jason saw me look at Zeek with discomfort and a bit of disdain. As to make me more comfortable Jason then said, "Zeek's harmless. Listen, if you're not in your element after half hour or so we'll leave. Okay?"

I did feel better when he said that. At the same time, I did come with him and didn't want to be a buzz-kill. I mean I would be pretty annoyed if my friend told me he wanted to leave as soon as I introduced him to my friends.

"Alright," I said and smiled as I looked on at Zeek twirling around under the dark night's sky.

Moments later another car pulled in to the park and stopped directly in front of Jason and I. It was a pearl white 2010 BMW 535i. I don't even need to go into the details of what this beauty had, as any BMW can speak for itself. *All the bells and whistles* is an understatement. Jason had a slight smile on his face as the doors of the beamer came open. I turned to his line of vision to see what made him smile, and when I did, I think I smiled too.

Two beautiful girls, maybe a year or two younger than us, step out from the beamer.

"Hey Jason, how are you?" Katlyn said in her soft voice as her and Ella walked toward us. If "all the bells and whistles" was an understatement for the car, it must have been an understatement for these two girls.

I was raised to lower my gaze. I was raised to address women with respect and be mindful that I had a sister. So, if I were to look at a female in a less than honorable way, then I would be accepting for that to be done to my baby sister by other guys. I couldn't have that. The thought of some guy sizing up my little sister makes me see red. I have had my fair share of bloodied knuckles for smart guys that thought it would be okay to disrespect my sister. They regretted it, all eight of them. Yes, I keep count. If there was one thing my father drilled in me, it was protectiveness over my sister.

"You are her guardian. Her protector. You are her *Abbas*, and she is your *Zaynab*. You understand?" My father would tell me as he grabbed my shoulders with his two rock solid palms. I would nod my head slowly in agreement.

"Yes sir." I would say, a soldier answering his commander. I grew up listening to the story of Ashura, the tragedy in which the Prophet Muhammad's grandson, Imam Hussain, and his band of seventy-two companions were massacred by the Umayyad caliphate's army of thirty thousand. Imam Hussain's women and children were taken as prisoners, whipped and tortured by the Umayyad soldiers from the desert plains of Karbala, to the city of Kufa, and on to the imperial palace in Damascus. The tale of the calamities, with its endless lessons of honor, chivalry, sacrifice and faith, would be told for centuries thereafter.

One of those stories would be that of Hussain's brother, Abbas, and his sister Zaynab. Abbas was their younger brother. A champion in battle and a chivalrous knight who trained under the sword of his father, Imam Ali, *the Commander of the Faithful*. Before he passed, Imam Ali would remind Abbas of his duty to protect his sister

Zaynab. Abbas made that his life's purpose. He would graciously fulfill that role until he was killed at the banks of the Euphrates River while he tried to retrieve water for Zaynab and the children, who had been deprived of water for three days.

Like Abbas, I would be my sister's guardian. I would be her protector. I promised to protect her and I always did. Whether I was successful in protecting myself, however, was a different story.

So, did I try to lower my gaze? Yes. Was I successful all the time? Absolutely not. That night I wasn't successful. And she, Ella, wasn't too bashful either.

"How's it going ladies?" Jason said as he opened his arms out anticipating the collegial embrace of their hugs.

"Girls I want to introduce you to my good friend Al. He's a gentleman and a beast, depending on how, when, and where, if you know what I mean?" Jason laughed and lightly jabbed my arm.

"Seriously?" I said to him under my breath already kind of embarrassed.

"What? Gentleman in the classroom, beast on the football field. That's all I'm saying. All-American right here."

Good save Jason.

"It's nice to meet you Al," said Katlyn, Jason's individual of interest it seemed.

Katlyn was tall, thin, and blonde. She looked like a model you would see on the cover of almost any magazine. She extended her hand to shake mine, as any person would do in a situation of meeting someone for the first time. Right? Not exactly.

This is where it can be awfully simple or horribly awkward. Remember the whole modesty, lowering of the gaze, respecting women spiel above? Well, I was also raised not to hug, shake hands with, or even high five girls in the same spirit. My mom would tell me, as early as elementary school, the difference in how I should behave and interact with boys and girls.

"Ali, my dear, I know you like girls," she would say to me as she buttoned up my shirt getting me ready for school. And I did. I showed my liking for girls at an early age. I didn't play the age-old playground game of boys vs. girls. I didn't think girls were "icky" and I wasn't afraid to get infected with "cooties". I was very friendly as a kid, especially with my female classmates. I was expressive. I gave too many hugs and I took many more. I liked girls. They liked me.

Things would have to change when innocence would shed, and innocence naturally fades with age. And when that age came my mom and dad gave me more than one talk.

"But you have to know that you can't just hug girls when you wish and please. You have to give people their space, especially with girls dear," my mother told me.

"What do you mean especially with girls?" I would ask almost offended. I was apprehensive of this emphasis.

"Well, don't you like girls differently than boys?" she asked.

"Yeah?" I answered unsure of where this was leading.

"Then you need to be considerate of that. You must show them even more respect and be especially good to them."

I wasn't satisfied with the answer and she could tell.

"You are like a chivalrous knight and ladies are royal princesses that should be treated as such. Just like you protect your sister you should protect other people's sisters too. You see?"

Mama caressed my cheek with her soft hands and smiled at me with her gentle eyes. She always made me feel like everything was possible and that everything would be okay.

"I see," I smiled back.

I saw my sister Emily as an innocent princess that must be honored and protected. I was a chivalrous knight and she was royalty. I felt that way and acted accordingly in many situations thereafter throughout our youth. But in this park with Jason and his friends, Ella and Katlyn, I wasn't feeling like a knight and they didn't gaze at me like royalty.

"He doesn't shake hands Katlyn, it's against his religious beliefs of modesty," Jason said to her with surprising eloquence as he swatted her hand playfully.

"Oh. You're not a prude, are you?" Katlyn snarled at me.

I knew I was blushing, I was sure of it. But thank God, I was veiled by the darkness of the night. Though embarrassed I managed to say, "Not at all," with some confidence.

"Then what are you?" Ella came closer to me and asked softly.

"He's yours," Jason said as he put his arm around Katlyn and both walked off giggling.

"I'm Ali. And you are?" I asked her as I gazed at her. It was hard to look away. She was stunning. Her silky smooth brown hair fell just past her shoulders and I could smell her soft floral fragrance as she walked in closer to me. She looked at me with her big hazel brown eyes. Even though it was dark out, I could see her so clearly. I could see the world in those spheres of hers, she didn't even know it.

"I'm Ella," she replied so softly it was close to a whisper.

"Since you don't shake hands, what do you do when you meet people?" Ella asked.

"Well it's not people in general, just with females," I replied but quickly realized how bad that sounded. "It's out of respect for the modesty of a lady that we greet her heart to heart instead of skin to skin." I placed my hand on my heart. "Like this," and gestured for her to do the same.

"I see. I get it. It's your way of acknowledgement," she said with her hand still on her chest. "Heart to heart, I like that. It's different, but I like it."

"I'm really not trying to be different. It's just a thing I was raised with, you know, my culture…"

"I respect it," she interrupted quietly. But she kept getting closer to me. She was wearing a fitted zip up hoodie on top of black yoga pants. I started wondering if she had just gotten back from the gym and admired how toned she looked. Then I thought if she looks this good in the dark, how would I be able to keep it together in broad daylight? I don't know if I would be able to pull this discussion of handshaking off. Ali. Focus. Stop wandering in your wonderful thoughts. Back to respect.

"And I respect you. That's the whole point," I said to her and looked away. I don't know if she knew how hard I was trying to be respectful and practice restraint.

"I want to be respected," she replied now standing only about a foot away from me. "So be chivalrous and walk me over there where we can sit down and talk about it," she said as she got on her tip toes and spoke to me face to face only a few inches apart.

"Sure! After you," I took one big step back and extended my hand gesturing for her to begin walking. Instead, she grabbed my hand and held it. She had a pretty tight grip so I couldn't pull away even if I wanted to. At that point, I wasn't so sure I wanted to.

I looked at her eyes wide.

"I thought you understood the whole thing about hand shaking?" I said looking at her hand and then looking back at her again.

"I'm not shaking your hand, I'm holding it," she said with a devilish smile.

I laughed. I felt a sense of comfort with her. But there was an eerie feel of regret creeping. I couldn't tell if it was because I knew what I was doing was wrong or what was about to come would be worse.

"You're bad," I said as I shook my head.

"You haven't seen anything yet Ali," she looked back at me again with that devilish smile of hers.

There was a small bench under a tree in the distance, quite secluded from the rest of the park. We walked over there and plotted ourselves down on that old wooden bench. Ella was still holding my hand; I had almost forgotten about it. She tilted her head back, resting it on the back of the bench as her hair would drop behind her.

"Do you ever just look up and stare at the stars?"

"Yeah, sure."

I tried to be cool in my response, but she didn't know that gazing at the stars is by far one of my favorite things to do, especially alone. I can sit outside on the grass for hours just looking at the stars and getting lost in the Milky Way. I like Milky Way chocolate very much by the way. Even though I did this alone, I didn't mind sharing the Milky Way with someone worthwhile – be it the galaxy or the chocolate.

"What do you think about when you look up at the stars?" She asked without turning away from the dark canvas.

"A lot of stuff I suppose," I answered reluctantly. I didn't know Ella. I wasn't ready to just start sharing the depths of my thoughts with her simply because she asked. If I couldn't guard my hands from Ella's reach, then I could at least guard my thoughts. But soon enough even that would fall prey to her.

Ella raised her head to look at me and said, "Ali don't be so guarded. Gaze at the stars with me and share your thoughts. I can tell you're deep and I'm deeper than you think. You can give me a chance."

I continued to look at the stars.

"Why do you gaze at the stars as you do?" I asked.

"I supposed because they're so beautiful. It's calming, you know." She responded as she turned her face back to the night's sky.

"I don't think so."

"You don't think the stars are beautiful?"

"Of course they are. I don't think that's why you look at them though."

"Why do I look at them then?" she asked me with intrigue in her voice.

"So you don't know why you look at them?" I asked teasing her.

"I do but you weren't satisfied with my response so I am asking you oh wise one!" she said as she bowed her head before me playfully mocking me.

"You don't gaze at the stars because you are amazed by them, you gaze at the stars because you are bewildered by the things you can do. You don't fix your eyes to the sky because it calms you, you look up because you're searching for yourself. You can't find yourself down here so you're looking up hoping you'll get lucky. It isn't the stars that twinkle, it is your eyes. It isn't the stars that shine, it is your heart of gold. And even though there are so many stars up there and so many people down here, there really is only one of you... just one."

My eyes were on the sky the whole time. I didn't look away. But the silence only grew louder. After a few moments I turned to her to see if I had mysteriously been left alone and spoken that just to my lonesome. But I noticed my hand was still being held, and she was still there. Ella looked at me with her eyes wide open. I couldn't read her face either because it was truly blank or it really was too dark to read at night.

"Ella?" I said.

"Who are you?" she asked me in a quiet voice as she looked me dead in the eyes.

"Did I say something wrong?" I asked in a soft voice.

"I wish you did," she said. "No one has ever said something like that to me. I mean it was poetic but... damn... where did you come from?"

"Well I've never received a compliment like that before so the feeling is mutual," I smiled. I lied. I have received compliments like that before, especially with regards to my poetry. But it was special from her. I liked Ella. I liked her in more than a few ways.

"I would very much like to kiss you right now," she told me.

"You barely know me Ella," I said in a weak defense.

"But you know me so well."

Before I could respond again she wrapped her hands around my neck and planted her lips on mine. Was I defenseless? No. I was twice her size. Could I have gotten her off me? Absolutely. Did I? No.

"If you're anything like your father then you're going to need to watch yourself ten times harder when it comes to women," my dad told me once as we ate peanut butter and banana sandwiches at the dinner table one evening. I was ten years old. And he had a point. I had developed a liking to women from the tender age of five. And they liked me too! I loved being around girls.

I had my first "girlfriend" when I was six. How did she become my girlfriend you may ask? I did what any other six-year-old would do. I gave her my fruit-roll-up and asked her to be my girlfriend. She said "Okay!" We high-fived and it was a done deal. Things didn't stay so innocent as I grew up and moved on to junior high, high school, and then college. My dad would give me constant reminders to stay on track. No matter how creative he was, it remained a struggle. Boy was it a struggle.

I never had a problem with getting girls' attention. My problem was keeping myself in check, so I didn't fall on the slippery slope to sin. When you hit that slippery slope it's hard to control yourself. You lose balance. You're on the slippery slope! Now control has varying levels and so does sin. You have to stop yourself from the smallest and most platonic sins as to not slip into the more dangerous ones. My dad taught me that. It can be a handshake, a hug, and even a gaze. You know what they say about the ripple effect of small things. With Ella I tried to at least be somewhat in control and not fall into every possible sin. That didn't last long. She was just too beautiful.

My father knew I wasn't like Joseph – not my cousin, rather Joseph the prophet. I couldn't turn my back to Ella as Joseph did with Zulaykha. I didn't have his strength or will power. That is why my father stressed the matter to me so much, as early as ten years old, even before I hit puberty.

"When an unmarried man and an unmarried woman are alone together, they're never alone, did you know that?" My father told me as we were building a wooden picnic table in our garage.

"Is it because God is always watching them?" My innocent ten-year-old self would answer courageously as I handed a hammer to my father.

"Good answer son. Yes. But in that alone-time they think they have, there is always a third wheel as company. He'll never leave them in peace. Whenever they meet, he's there. But they don't even know."

"Who is it baba?" I asked, my eyes wide with intrigue.

"*Shaitan*," he said so quietly it was as if he was only mouthing the word. Satan.

I thought I would never forget that. It was etched in my mind. You're never really alone. That night with Ella, though, I did forget. I thought our company was merely a beautiful canvas of the night's starry sky. I forgot my father's directives and wisdom. But was forgetfulness here a conscious one? Did I want to forget? Did I choose to forget? I think so. The pleasure of the moment and the curiosity of how far I would go this time plagued me. It was almost a thrill, a dangerously silent one as well. It didn't scream out at you, it was guised with poetry, subtle romance, and platonic discourse. In reality, it was all a façade and the roads led to the same dismal end.

That night with Ella, things got out of hand to say the least. It wasn't the first time I let things get out of hand like that, as I did have my fair share of "fun" in college. That fun was usually short-lived, fleeting moments of pleasure accompanied by deep feelings of guilt; that would nonetheless fade before the next opportunity presented itself. Throughout college, I never did drink or do hard drugs even though it always seemed to present itself. The euphoric sensation or "high" from those substances never lured me. What did lure me was a woman's touch, the smell of her hair, and the softness of her skin. As the most beautiful of God's creation, women were surely my weakness.

I didn't plan to become so intimate with this girl I had just met. Nor was it of my planning or preference to do so in such an improper way. There were other ways I suppose. But that required a more serious sense of restraint. It required patience and strength. But I didn't have that. And I chose to forget. I chose to ignore what was righteous, even though I thought I knew it so well. I sinned when I had other options, and I enjoyed it. I closed my eyes and I chose to forget. In those moments, I chose Ella over everything else.

Our pleasure though was suddenly interrupted by the shrieking of a newly familiar voice.

"You love birds must be thirsty!"

Ella jumped off me, startled by the company that had unexpectedly joined us. It wasn't Shaitan but it sure was close. Zeek stood in front of us snickering while Jason and Katlyn trailed behind him.

"Seriously Zeek?! You scared the crap out of me," Ella said as she quickly grabbed her shirt off the ground to cover her bare chest. Apparently I was shirtless as well.

"Relax Ella Bella… I got you guys drinks to cool off your steamy bodies…" Zeek slithered and bit his lips seductively. He spoke to her like he knew her or something. This guy was something else.

"I don't drink," we both said at the same time. We looked at each other and smiled. Who would have known that two people who barely knew each other could be so in sync?

"You guys are adorable!" Katlyn came from behind and said dotingly.

"Stop it Katie," Ella sharply replied.

"What's wrong with her?" She turned to Jason.

"You ruined a moment that's what's wrong," Ella exclaimed.

"A moment huh? Looks like you guys had a lot more than a moment. Didn't I promise you wouldn't regret coming out tonight Al?" Jason said and gave me a wink.

"Cool off your moment with a drink. I promise no alcohol. It's just root bear. Scout's honor." Zeek handed us the two plastic red cups and gave us a scout's salute.

My mouth did feel dry and I thought that if it was alcohol Jason would warn me against it. He's done that in the past so I thought there was no issue. No harm no foul right?

"This tastes off… like it's flat or something," I said as I sipped at the red cup. I hated flat pop. It was an abomination. If it's flat, then it has no fizz. If it has no fizz it does not pop. If it doesn't pop, then it's not pop. It lost its whole identity. With no identity, what's your use? You have none. There is no use keeping around flat pop, it's not like it's going to miraculously turn back to full fizz. At times, that's how I felt about myself. Flat pop. But I stuck around. And this red cup of flat pop stuck around with me. I ignored my feeling of distaste and drank the whole cup out of thirst.

That is the last thing I remember. Drinking from that cup that Zeek gave me. I knew Zeek was bad news.

Now it was past dawn and getting close to sunrise. I must have been knocked out for a few hours. I searched my pockets and couldn't find my wallet, my keys, or my phone. I frantically looked around where I was laying, searching the blades of grass with my fingers, getting the dirt underneath my finger nails, and staining the legs of my jeans in green. I jogged back to the bench where I remember Ella and I sat. Luckily, my phone was right underneath the bench. I guess it fell out of my hands after Ella and I paid tribute to Venus.

I unlocked my phone to find only two percent of battery life left. I called the first person that came to mind whenever I needed anything, whenever anyone in the family needed anything really. *Adam.*

3. ADAM THE SAVIOR

What I love about Adam is that no matter what, and no matter when, he always answers his phone. There wasn't a time when I called Adam that he ignored my call or even missed it by chance. It's practically part of his brand as a person. This wasn't the first time I called Adam for help.

One fall, I visited a friend of mine in Chicago. I decided to take the train. I packed a small bag with the basics, drove to the train station, parked my car and barely made it on time before the train took off. It was a 6:15 morning ride and I was getting off from a night shift.

I found a seat toward the front of the train. It was interesting because barely anyone was there. You would assume that people would want front row seats, wouldn't you? Well I guess these passengers didn't. There were only a few people in the cabin so luckily I could have my space there. I threw my bag in the upper level compartment over the seats, took my jacket off, and got settled in. I find train rides to be particularly relaxing. I'm getting to my destination while I can read a book, work off my laptop, or just stare out the window and admire the world. I wish the rest of life could be like this. You sit and admire while someone else does the brunt work of driving you to your destination. Wouldn't that be great?

I crossed my arms, put up my feet on the seat next to me, and looked out the window of the moving train. Leaving the city sights of buildings and homes, the train passed through woods and small bodies of water. I wondered as I watched the ever-changing leaves of the trees. How many colors does each tree experience? Green, red, orange, yellow, and colors in between. It was such a beautiful scene. As the weather changes, their colors do too. Is it their expression to how they feel about what is happening around them? As humans we have many colors too. I watched as the sun's rays glistened the small lakes and river streams so majestically. The water looked so clear and pure, even though it was only glimpses from my vantage on this passing train.

After a good five hours I arrived in Chicago. My friend was waiting for me at the station. From that point on and for the next 48 hours, we had a blast. Eating, sightseeing, bike riding through the city, we did it all. It ended too soon and before you knew it, I found myself back at Union Station for my return ride home. Would I do it again? Definitely. It was a great time and it was cheap! $35 for a roundtrip train ride? Heck yeah I'll take it. Problem is I had read it wrong. It was $35 for the ticket there, one-way.

When I went to Union Station at the time I thought I had reserved for my trip, I didn't have an actual ticket for the train. I really don't know how I overlooked that. So, I went up to the counter and explained my situation to the uninterested ticket clerk.

"Sorry, we're all sold out," she said apathetically.

"When is the next available train?" I asked.

"All of the trains today are sold out. You're going to have to wait until tomorrow."

I had to be back before tomorrow. I had class and work. I found myself alone at Union Station. I had no return ticket home. It was 1pm and I would have to wait until tomorrow to get on the next available ride. The friend I was visiting in Chicago was already on his way to the airport flying out to Spain for a study-abroad program. I wasn't going to tell my family, what an embarrassment. I didn't have any friends that were willing to drive several hours to pick me up and drive me back.

And that was a lot to ask of someone anyways. I felt defeated.

My phone vibrates in my pocket. I'm getting a phone call. I pulled my phone out of my jean pocket to see my savior's name and picture on my home screen. *Adam.*

"Hey cousin!" he said on the phone.

"Hey Adam," I said in a low voice.

"Just checking up on you. What's up?"

"Nothing much really," I replied.

"Why do you sound down? What's wrong?"

I explained to him the situation I was in and how I really didn't know what to do.

"I'm doing some work in Kalamazoo. I can be there in a couple hours."

My heart was elated but I felt really bad. "No cousin, I can't have you do that. That's too much man." I genuinely said.

"Don't worry habibi, you're good. I got you." No one knew what had happened other than him. He picked me up, we had a deep dish slice, and we headed back home.

When I found myself that cold morning stranded in Hines Park, dizzy and unsure of what had happened, I had Adam to save me again. "I'm on my way," he said without hesitation when I told him where I was. Without giving him many details, he understood and acted. He was decisive. He was dependable. He was courageous. He was Adam.

He pulled in to the park in less than ten minutes from the moment we ended our phone call. I hurried towards the car and climbed inside to the passenger's seat. He drove a newer Ford F-150. He didn't work construction but he sure did haul a lot of stuff for people. When I asked him, "Out of all the nice cars you could get yourself, why did you get an F-150? I mean it's nice don't get me wrong but do you need it?"

"I don't need it. Other people do," he said with a smile. That was Adam, always thinking about what others needed and how he could calmly be there when they did. But I think he was fed up with me, not because I needed something, but because I didn't know what I needed.

"Thanks for coming Adam," I said as he began to reverse out of the parking lot.

He didn't say, "You're welcome." He didn't say anything. It was a few minutes of silence that spoke in the car.

"This isn't you," Adam broke the silence.

I didn't respond.

"You call me at 6am to pick you up from Hines Park? Really?"

I looked outside the car window as if I was searching for an answer because I sure as hell didn't have it.

"You don't do this kind of crap Ali," he continued. "Who's calling the shots right now? Because it isn't you."

"What do you mean?"

"I mean if you were calling the shots in your life right now, you wouldn't be waking up in the middle of a public park at the break of dawn."

He was right. But I was still a bit hazy and my brain wasn't processing things as quickly as it normally did.

"It's a girl isn't it?" he asked almost certain of himself.

"What's a girl?"

"Calling the shots for you. The reason I'm picking you up from this damn park." Adam snapped his fingers at me twice. "Wake up brother!"

I was in a daze. I was struggling to stay awake.

"What happened? Talk to me Ali."

If there was anyone I could talk to it was Adam. Even after putting myself in this embarrassing situation, he would be the person I could talk to. So I began to talk.

"I was hanging out with Jason and a couple of his friends."

"Okay that was your first mistake... carry on," Adam interrupted.

Adam wasn't fond of Jason. He knew his older brother, not the best guy around town. He was known to party hard and experiment a little too often with drugs. But Jason wasn't like him. Apparently, I was wrong.

"These two girls show up and one of them was really into me. I tried to keep my distance but it didn't work," I continued.

"It didn't work or you didn't try hard enough?" Adam interrupted again.

"Bro, you know what I mean. I'm a guy and she's an attractive girl. I tried not to fall. I failed. We hit it off. Until Zeek barged in with his stupid music and drinks."

"You were drunk Ali?" Adam turned to me with disdain.

"No man you know I don't drink. He was drunk. He was drinking."

"So you didn't drink anything while you were there?"

"Of course not..." I paused. "Actually no. I did. But it was just pop. It did taste weird though," I said scratching my head.

"Weird how?" Adam was looking at me trying to pull answers out of me faster than I could.

"I don't know. I thought it was flat, but come to think of it, it was just different. And I don't remember anything after that."

Adam abruptly pulled to the side of the road.

"They spiked your drink Ali."

"Spiked it? Spiked it how?" I asked bewildered by the concept.

"I would guess they gave you Roofies or something equivalent. They likely grounded the substance and mixed it in your drink when you weren't looking. Something strong enough to knock you out after a few minutes but not too strong where it doesn't kill you. They're not that stupid."

"What do you mean? Are you serious?!" I got even dizzier thinking about it.

"Your buddies Zeek and Jason. They're no good man. What's Jason been up to lately? Has he found a job yet? Or is he still hitting the streets like his brother?"

"I don't know."

"This guy Zeek. I've heard of him. You may think he's dumb but it's all a show. He's that random 'party animal' that shows up to gatherings. Most people in the party don't know him but he comes off as just a funny drunk kid. He waits until people's guards are down and he steals from them."

I chuckled. "That seems a little too sophisticated for Zeek," I said almost mocking Adam's theory.

"Oh yeah? Where's your wallet Ali?"

I looked away in shame.

"Exactly. Not with you. It's with Zeek the Beak."

"The Beak? They call him that?"

"Yeah. Because he picks people's pockets as quick as a bird picks at worms."

"You really know these guys, huh?"

"I have to know everyone. You know that Ali."

He really did know everyone.

Adam was more aggressive with me than usual. Though I was kind of offended, I was too embarrassed to make a point out of it. He was usually calm and cool when he talked. He had this suave, this swag, this chill that just made you feel good. But carrying on the energy he had with me at the hospital, to being picked up in his car, it was definitely different. One thing's for certain. He wasn't the variable. I was.

Adam put the car back in drive, his tires turned up the muddy ground, and he was back on the road. Adam's truck was a beast. He could go off-roading in the woods if he wanted to with that thing. But no off-roading now, let's get back on track. The dramatic effect of stopping on the roadside did its part.

"So what are you going to do?" Adam asked me.

"I'm going to call Jason."

I dialed his number and waited for it to ring.

"He already has you blocked Ali," Adam said.

He was right! It went straight to voicemail. I tried again a couple more times. Same deal.

"Maybe his phone is dead," I said half-heartedly.

"He's tight on money now Ali. The first thing you need to do when you get home is report all your credit cards stolen. They already went on a shopping spree at some of the 24/hour places, probably Meijers. They didn't time it well since they're rookies and they're hungry."

"Hungry?"

"Not for food. For money. Money that isn't theirs to pay for drugs they shouldn't be taking," he said placing both hands on the steering wheel. I could tell he was getting a little upset. Adam was involved in this scene a while back. So he knew it pretty well. He knew the streets. Not that he did drugs, but he befriended a few guys that ran some low-key operations. He helped keep them out of trouble, but was part of the scene nonetheless. He was an extra pair of eyes and ears, along with a brain that could assess opportunities and risks much better than they did.

He left the scene when one of his buddies was killed in the process. An exchange gone wrong, a few heated words, teenagers packing heat and bam. Adam's friend gets shot and loses his life at the tender age of twenty-two. Adam looked up to him. But it was when he was down on the ground, looking down at his bloodied body that Adam realized he had to grow up quick before he'd find himself in the same spot. Adam was only nineteen when he saw his friend die before his eyes. He was there, hovered over his friend's body, trying to stop the bleeding with his bare hands as he screamed out for help. He never told me the story himself but I've heard it from quite a few people, family too.

"You listening to me cousin?"

"Yeah, report the credit cards stolen."

"No, you don't know that for sure and you don't want to go through the police reporting process. It's a headache for you. Report them lost. They'll issue you new cards within the week."

"What about Jason and the others?"

"Forget about Jason," Adam paused. "You mean the girl?"

"Yeah…" I said hesitantly.

"Ali, they robbed you."

"I know I sound gullible but I don't think she was a part of it."

"Does it really matter to you right now? You got robbed. You're distant from your family. Your mom is in the hospital. You're all over the place and you're thinking about this random girl you hit it off with in the middle of the night in Hines Park?!"

"How did you know I hit it off with her?" I turned to Adam and asked.

"Really Ali?" he asked annoyed.

"Seriously? How would you know?" I was honestly weirded out by how accurate he was.

"Because I know you. I know how far you would go and where you would stop. I know where you struggle and where you fail. I know what you see as right and what you see as wrong. I know how you were raised and even with all that your dad taught you, I know what you've really taken and what you haven't. Is that good enough for you?"

"I suppose," I looked away in shame again.

"And you basically told me she made you a happy camper soon as you got in the car doofus!"

I punched him on the shoulder. We both laughed. Adam was the man. He could tell it to you straight and you couldn't stay mad at him. You knew he understood you. He wasn't judgmental. He wasn't condescending. He went through the motions. He was down in the gutter. He picked himself up and he elevated himself.

I wanted to do that for myself. I wanted a change. I needed a change. I knew the principles. I knew what I had to do in life, but I didn't feel it. I didn't really *know* it. It was all theory to me. But the passion and emotion behind the principle wasn't there.

"I think I need to go to *Hajj*," I said looking out the windshield at the road ahead.

"Is that so? Why?" Adam asked intrigued by what seemed to be a random statement.

"I need to change."

"But you're not a bad guy," he said almost teasingly.

"I want better."

"You just have your priorities out of order Ali. You don't need to go to Hajj to figure it out."

"But isn't that what helped you change?"

Adam went to Hajj the year after his friend was killed. He was twenty. His life seemed to turn around after that. He became focused and determined to do the right thing for himself and his family. I thought that I could do the same thing for myself.

"Hajj didn't help me change. It gave me a fresh start. I needed the fresh start. What helped me change was my willpower." Adam became very serious.

"I didn't just *want* to change, I *needed* to change."

"I'm trying to get there cousin. But I don't want to hit rock bottom."

"You woke up on the lawn of Hines Park, that sounds like rock bottom to me!" he punched me on my shoulder and we both laughed again. I never imagined I could laugh about this. With anyone else I wouldn't. I would be in tears. But with Adam, there was hope. There was ease. I mean it was Adam.

"You do need a change. You need to get away and clear your head. But it can't be to California or some place on a beach."

"I'm not looking for a vacation. I need to find some answers. I know they're there but I need to know I can find them for sure wherever it is I go. That's why I thought of Hajj."

"You need to go on *Ziyara*."

"Ziyara?"

"Najaf. Karbala. Iraq. You need to have a conversation with the best of the best. Yeah. You need to go to Ziyara. You'll find your answers there."

"Baba is from Iraq."

"I know. Better reason to go. Maybe you can see some of your relatives too."

"My dad hasn't been there in years."

"And you haven't been there ever."

"Ziyara?"

"Didn't you just want to go to Hajj? At least this won't cost you seven grand." Adam chuckled.

"Seven grand?! You paid seven grand?"

"Nah. When I went it was like five. Inflation in the Middle East has been on the rise. Don't you listen to NPR?"

I hadn't listened to any news lately, let alone NPR, but that was beside the point. The more I thought of it the more it made sense to me, especially the fact that it hadn't been a consideration before. The pleasant surprise of the idea grew more and more appealing.

"I think that's what I'll do." I said nodding my head slowly as I continued to look at the road ahead.

"Yeah. I think it'll do it for you. Two people I'll connect you with, one you already know and one you will get to know and won't regret that you did."

"Who?" I said with genuine interest.

"The first is Hadi. We grew up with him. Great guy. He goes on Ziyara all the time. Not with a group or anything. He does his own thing and knows his way around. You'll enjoy your time with him, he's a character."

I remember Hadi as kids growing up. He was this corky humorous kid who always had a smile on his face. He came from a good family, both his parents were middle class professionals, but he was never spoiled. His parents gave him a lot of attention but not many toys. I remember his dad once saying, "Things don't give you love, people do." How do I remember that? I have no idea. I guess it stuck with me.

"Hadi's cool. I didn't realize he was so religious. He doesn't come off that way," I said.

"Come off that way? What's *that way*?"

Adam pulled in to the new Tim Hortons erected on the right side of Ford Rd. He needed his morning fix.

"You want something?" Adam asked me.

"No, I'm good. I need to get some sleep."

"I'll get my medium dark roast coffee, double-double, in a large cup please," Adam spoke into the outdoor menu's built-in speakerphone system.

"Coming right up Adam," the girl on the other side of the speakerphone replied cheerfully.

"She knows your name?" I asked.

Adam smiled.

"How does she know your name?" I asked more directly.

"Same order at the same time of the morning, 6:55am, every day for the past ninety days… they should know my middle name by now."

I chuckled.

We pulled up to the next window and Adam's steaming cup of coffee delight was already waiting for him.

"Here you go Adam." The girl opened the window and handed Adam the hot cup with a smile.

"Thanks Nadia." He smiled right back. She closed the window and he drove off.

"You didn't pay," I observed and said out loud.

Adam chuckled as he sipped his coffee.

"And you knew her name too!" I realized and spat out as if making some huge discovery.

"So what did you mean by 'he doesn't come off that way'?" Adam asked inquisitively reverting back to the original subject.

"Who's the second person you said I would meet there?" I reminded Adam.

"Yes! I almost forgot. That would be the *Sayyid*." Adam replied. Sayyid was a reference to a person who was from the lineage of the Prophet Muhammad. So it really could have been anybody.

"Which sayyid?" I asked.

"The Sayyid."

"What is he a grand scholar or something like I'm supposed to know what sayyid you're talking about. And even if that was the case, most of them are Sayyids too," I responded in annoyance.

"Bro, it's *The Sayyid*."

"Which one?! There's thousands of them, especially in Najaf!" I exclaimed.

Adam sighed and looked outside his window.

"Honestly, I just don't remember his name."

I cracked up laughing.

"Am I bad?" he asked gasping for air as we laughed hysterically.

"You're the worst!" I replied.

"Don't worry, I have his number and so does Hadi. I'll get you his name. But you're going to just call him Sayyid anyway."

"I feel much better now," I said sarcastically.

"You should. You're going to meet a man that can teach you the meaning of life just by you looking at him."

I waited for Adam's que to laugh again, my mouth and eyes open ready to burst out another hilarious laugh. But he didn't laugh. He was serious.

"No kidding?"

"No joke. He's the real deal. I think this will be great for you."

I nodded as we pulled into my driveway.

"Crap I forgot I have like nine missed calls from my dad." I was getting nervous again.

"What are you going to tell him?" Adam asked.

"I don't know. What should I say?"

"I'll take care of it for you. I'll talk to him."

Then my dad appeared behind the screen door of the front entrance of our house. He was in a white V-Neck and black Nike jogging pants. He crossed his arms and waited for me to come out of the car.

"Come on, let's have breakfast." Adam opened the car door and gestured for me to do the same and we walked toward the front door.

"Sabahil Kheir Ammu!" Good Morning Uncle. Adam shook my dad's hand and embraced him as he greeted him in Arabic.

"Sabahil Noor Adam," my dad responded coldly as he looked at us. Though his response was a "Morning of Light," it didn't seem to shine so brightly in those moments.

"I am so sorry I'm bringing Ali back home so late, or so early actually! We both fell asleep and his phone was under his seat. He picked it back up in the car and we're here now. *Samihnee* please," Adam asked for forgiveness as he put his hands together like a Christian prayer.

"It's okay, come on inside it's cold out." He grabbed Adam by the arm and pulled him inside.

"Great, I'll whip us up some breakfast." Adam responded as he smiled at me with a nod of success.

"It better be as good as it usually is Adam, your uncle is hungry this morning." My dad said as he walked inside through the living room and to the kitchen.

Adam patted me on the back guiding me into my own house and said as he followed him, "I got you Ammu, don't I always?"

This guy Adam. He saved me. Again. What do I call him? My friend in need? My hero? No. He was more than that. He was godsend. He was my savior...

I would have more than these instances to thank him for.

We walked into the kitchen and Adam got started on his famous mushroom omelets with *Halal* — the Muslim equivalent of Kosher — turkey bacon. I went to the bathroom to wash my face so I could stay awake for another hour or so. I turned the handle and watched the stream of water run out of the silver faucet. I splashed my face with cold water and felt a rush of alertness come to me. Yup, that will do the trick. It's good for your skin too they say. Well some say otherwise, but it is said.

I looked up at the reflection of my face in the mirror of the medicine cabinet hanging above the sink in front of me. I looked into my own eyes. If I could get lost in the eyes of another, I could swim for days in my own. Selfish? Possibly. But who is closer to me than me? No one. As I stared I expected the emptiness I had been seeing for some time now. But it seemed a bit different. It wasn't the same. It felt a bit less empty. It was as if my proverbial empty cup had been filling up, not with much of course. I gained a few droplets... a few droplets of hope.

"I am going," I whispered.

4. THE PIONEER PRISONER

Before going on Ziyara, Adam told me that I needed to do some introspection and reflect on what made me, me. "You need to think more than you usually do. Not in the sense of worrying about things, but more so about the meaning behind things," he told me.

I sat down in those few weeks I had preparing for my trip thinking about the experiences I have gone through over the years and the lessons I should have learned from those who are wiser than me. I thought about the things that should have shaped me into who I am today, and how my own lacking may have molded who I am. One particular reflection stuck with me more than others. It was one inspired by the Hajj, my father.

Growing up, my father told me that if I wanted to be a man I should look at the struggles of others and ask myself if I could carry their burdens instead of my own. If the answer was "No," then I would be lacking in my personal strength and courage.

"Are you not strong enough to take on another responsibility?" my father would ask me.

If the answer was "Yes," then I wasn't looking hard enough at their burden.

"You should not belittle the struggles that people go through, you do not understand their burden until you walk in their shoes."

Any straightforward answer to the question was wrong. It required more forethought and contemplation, rather than haste and quick judgments. That was what my father was trying to teach me. But, of course, I wouldn't see it until going through the motions myself. Still, his words would resonate with me for years to come. He planted the seed. I just had to water it.

When I was about twenty-one, a friend of mine – Raed – unknowingly helped provide me an opportunity to realize the lesson my father was trying to teach me in my youth. Raed's nickname was Red. We all called him "Red" for two reasons. One, he had thick curly red hair. Though his family was originally from southern Iraq, the kid practically looked Irish.

Two, that's how teachers pronounced it since elementary school, they couldn't annunciate the two syllables "Ra-id" if their life depended on it. Why his parents didn't spell it with an "i" you may ask. Well, then his name would have been Raid. It was going to be an invasion or pesticide, both ways the little red head kid was losing. He wasn't bothered too much by it, Red was a cool nickname anyway.

Whenever I think about Red's predicament or any other Arab kid's name troubles, I find myself thankful for the Arabic name my parents chose for me – Ali. The Champ made things simple for us by being the Greatest, so eventually the whole world had to say his name and respect it.

I grew up watching VCR tapes my dad had recorded of Muhammad Ali's fights. I watched him elegantly dance around his opponents and taunt them with his speed and agility. Sonny Liston, Joe Louis, Floyd Patterson, Cleveland Williams, Ernie Terrell, George Foreman and Joe Frazier. They all felt his presence, especially as he stood over them in victory. And even if they did not initially want to respect him or his new chosen name, as opposed to his Anglican name Cassius Clay, they would be forced to by the mere humility of defeat. Through that boxing ring he would allow his name, Muhammad Ali, to echo throughout America and the four corners of the world. I shared that victorious name.

So Red volunteered at a local Muslim charity that sent Islamic books for inmate converts at the state penitentiary. I wasn't doing much at that time. It was my junior year and during my winter semester I was only taking about 13 credit hours, half of which were complete blow-offs. Since I had some extra time to spare, I decided to help him out and do some good with my life. I learned the system and how they took orders and requests for specific books from the inmates. Normally they sent the books by mail. There was one inmate that ordered books every single month, usually three to four books too. The system was that you could order as many books as you wanted so long as you had completed and shipped back the books you already had. So this guy was knocking out these books left and right, not leaving a page unturned. Marking, highlighting, underlining, and leaving notes in the margins and all. One day I had the bright idea to hand deliver one of his orders.

The state penitentiary was about an hour away from where I lived. I had to make an appointment, which wasn't too hard. I made the appointment and before I knew it the date came. As I was about to head out to the prison, my phone vibrated in my pocket. Red's name showed up on my cellphone's black screen.

"Hey Red," I answered.

"Salaam bro," Red replied. He always greeted me with the Muslim greeting of "Peace", even if I didn't.

"Salaam. What's up man?"

"You sure you don't want me to come up with you to the state penitentiary?"

"Yeah man, don't worry about it. I'm sure it'll be fine. Plus, you're not on the appointment so they won't let you in."

"You're right," Red said. "But you know even if you just want me to come up for the ride. I'm ready to go."

Red was a nice kid. He always thought about his friends before himself. I appreciated his gesture, but I really wanted to do this on my own. I didn't mind the drive alone.

"I'm good Red. Thanks though buddy. I'll see you later today *inshallah*." God willing.

"Alright. If you need anything text me."

"Sounds good. *Salaam*."

The drive wasn't bad at all. I got there before I knew it. It was about an hour of open road outlined by thick woods. The drive was relaxing, almost therapeutic. I didn't think about the meeting with the inmate and what to expect. I just drove. My mind was clear. I was calm. I felt good.

I arrived and parked in the prison parking lot under the sign labeled "Visitors' Parking". The place was guarded like a fort. Uniformed officers with machine guns or snipers, I couldn't tell from the distance. Plus, I'm nearsighted. Or farsighted. I always get the two mixed up. I can't see things at a distance without my glasses. Nonetheless, I'm almost always without my glasses.

I walked cautiously into the prison facility, passing through the security gates and coming up to the check-in desk near the entrance.

"Hi, how are you? I have an appointment to visit a Mr. Hakeem Williams," I said with a pleasant smile to the officer at the check-in desk. Separating us was a thick sheet of glass with a round speaker phone in the middle of it.

The officer behind the glass didn't seem to be having a good day so I guess I wasn't going to be reciprocated with the same pleasant smile.

"What's your name sir?"

"Ali."

"I don't have an 'Ollie' on the visiting list."

"Are you sure? I scheduled my appointment as directed on the website, calling in and confirming two weeks in advance." I wasn't going to come all the way here and just be turned away now.

"No 'Ollies' on my list sorry sir. You're going to have to schedule another appointment and come back in two more weeks."

"Seriously?" I was livid.

I turned around, placed my hands on my head and took a deep breath. Then it clicked.

"Sir. I just want to make sure you have the spelling of my name correctly. It is A-L-I. Apple. Lion. Indigo. Ali."

I smiled, grinding my teeth away trying to stay cool.

"Let me double check that." He put his reading glasses on and looked through his computer database, clicking and typing away as if there were a hundred letters in my name. Three letters I had. That's all.

"Ah, yes. We got you here Ali. Just sign in here." He handed me a clipboard which I quickly took and signed my name away. What I was signing to, I had no idea. But I sure did sign.

"That officer down the hall will lead you through the gates and sit you down with Inmate 1412."

"Thank you, sir. I greatly appreciate your patience."

"Mm-hmm," he replied.

That irked me. What is that? What is a "mm-hmm"? Is it a phrase? No. Is it a word? No. It's a response that basically says you're not worth me giving you a real response composed of vocabulary, so here's a grunt for you. These small things drive me crazy. Call it a pet-peeve if you'd like but to me it's more of a principle. I greet you with words and candor, give me back the same. When I start communicating with non-words then go on and have a field day with your grunts, moans, groans, and mumbles.

I walked down the hallway and was escorted by Officer Johnson, an African-American guard, who seemed to be in a much better mood than the last.

He smiled and said, "How are you sir?"

"I'm good, how are you?"

"Great. Follow me. We'll go through this next security screening and I'll show you where you'll be meeting with Hakeem."

"Thank you, sir," I said sincerely.

"Don't mention it boss," he replied with a smile.

As we walked forward I decided to ask him something that was bothering me since I left the window with the other guard. No, not that he didn't know how to say "you're welcome."

"Why is it that the other guard called Hakeem 'Inmate 1412', but you called him by his name — more specifically by his first name?"

Johnson slowed his pace and walked beside me, as if what he was going to say had to be in closer physical proximity.

"Hakeem is a good guy. A great guy actually. A lot of the guards here don't like him though because he's smarter than they are. He doesn't need to be in this hell-hole." Johnson paused and looked around.

I read up on Hakeem's public criminal record before scheduling to visit him. I wanted to know what kind of convict I was going to be sitting across. Was he a murderer? A rapist? A drug dealer? I had to know. After going through the motions with Red he was able to get me his record. He's done it before for family and friends. It's not a complicated process but he knew how to do it so why attempt and fail myself? Turns out that Hakeem was convicted for a few gang-related crimes including a felony firearm possession, transportation of narcotics, and aggravated assault. Apparently, the guy had a past. I wasn't going to judge though, even though I kind of already did.

"His conviction and his sentencing was bull," Johnson whispered to me. "His judge was a Class-A jerk, and I know the judges." He looked around again to make sure we were still alone and no one was listening.

"He should have been out of here years ago, but he's rubbed a few important people the wrong way and will be stuck here for years to come."

"Wow. That's terrible." I said pondering the thought of being imprisoned for additional years merely because I upset someone in a position of power.

"Who did he upset?" I asked.

"Question is: who didn't he upset?"

"Is there any way for him to get out sooner? Good behavior? Extra hours of work in the system?"

Johnson shook his head.

"He's the most well-behaved inmate we have here in this prison. That's now. But when he got here he was angry. He's done with that part of himself. He learned his lesson. He knows his mistakes. He's not bothered by this place anymore though."

I looked around with a face close to disgust. Bare walls that haven't been painted in decades but occasionally decorated by human feces. The grungy stench of hundreds, maybe even thousands, of inmates filled the air. Rows upon rows of prison bars and orange jumpsuits is all you could see.

"Who wouldn't be bothered by this?"

"A man with no fear." Johnson smiled again.

"What do you mean?"

"You'll see."

Before I knew it, we were in front of the visiting room area and Hakeem was sitting on a table waiting for me. He didn't seem to be wasting his time though. He sat with his legs crossed, a book in his palms, and reading with large framed glasses hanging from the tip of his nose.

"Hakeem your visitor is here." Officer Johnson introduced me and walked away. He went into an observing room close by where guards watched the inmates behind a glass wall.

"Salaamu Alaykum, I'm Ali," I said and extended my hand toward Hakeem.

"Wa Alaykum Asalaam, I know who you are," he said as he removed his reading glasses and placed them on the table. He stood up from his seat and shook my extended hand. Oh boy was he tall. And he had quite the grip. His palms resembled more of rock than they did of flesh. It didn't seem like Hakeem had many days of "soft" labor before he came here.

"You know me?" I replied shocked by the idea that he knew me. How did he know me? I've never met him before in my life. How would he know me?

"Yes. They let us know who is coming to visit us before visiting hours," he replied.

"Oh." I felt so stupid.

Hakeem chuckled.

He was a big guy. But he wasn't scary big. He didn't seem like a criminal. He had what I remember an elderly African American woman told me I had... *kind eyes*.

"I brought you your books," I said as I placed the two books on the table and slid them over to him on that smooth laminate surface. Hakeem's face lit up. He looked like a kid in a candy store.

"Oh man! Thank you Ali, you just made my day! I've been waiting for these two for some time now." He grabbed the books and began flipping through them examining their contents. Glasses back on.

"I've never seen someone so excited to read books," I said with a smile looking at the book he was flipping through.

"Books are the gateway to the soul. A life without books is like a life unlived," Hakeem replied without taking his eyes off the book in his hands.

"Well a lot of people live fine without books. I mean even in college most people get by without even cracking open a book." I knew a lot of people like that. I would have done the same, but I majored in history. And I actually enjoyed reading. It took me to a different place when I didn't like where I was at.

"Get by?" Hakeem looked up at me.

"Yeah. Get by. A lot of people are able to do that."

"Do you know Socrates?" Hakeem asked me.

"Sure. Greek philosopher."

"Do you know that he was sentenced to death by the Greek state for two crimes?"

"No, I didn't," I really had no idea. I guess as a person who studied history I should have known that.

"Socrates was not only a philosopher; he was a game-changer. He was changing society with his ways of thinking. He was building a culture of reading, writing, questioning, and active contemplation. He had such a profound impact on people. The ruling class in Athens didn't like Socrates or his philosophies though. So they charged him with two crimes against society."

"Really? What did they charge him with?" I asked bewildered by the ordeal.

"For one 'impiety'," Hakeem gestured quotation marks with his fingers, "And secondly, for corrupting the youth of Athens."

He went on describing the colorful details of the trial and the politics behind Socrates' charges in Athens. For a few minutes I honestly was not listening to the content of his speech. I couldn't. I was just so taken aback by the situation I found myself in. I was sitting in a prison with this inmate across from me talking about Socrates and ancient Greece. I was fascinated to say the least.

"And all of his inspiration and insight came from where? Where do you think?" Hakeem pulled me back into the discussion and out from my fascination.

"Where?" I responded abruptly.

"Where else? Books." He picked the book back up and began examining it again.

"Makes sense," I said as I looked around the visiting room. I didn't know what else I should say. What would be appropriate to ask him? I didn't want to talk about why he was in prison. That would be inappropriate and rude. I would hate for someone to bring up my past, especially when I am constantly being reminded of it by the mere fact of where I lived. I wasn't going to go there. But Hakeem noticed my awkwardness in my low hum and my looking about.

"Why did you come visit me, Ali?" He asked with his glasses lowered.

"I guess I thought you would like the company," I replied. Why did I say that? Doesn't that sound condescending? Crap.

"Because you suppose it could get lonely in a place like this, right?"

"Yes! I would hate to be here." Damn it. Say something right Ali. You're usually more articulate than this.

"But that's not why you're here though," Hakeem asserted.

"What do you mean?" I replied.

"You're here in search for something. You couldn't find it in yourself so you're looking for it in others." Hakeem was looking straight at me. It felt like he was looking straight through me actually. I looked back at him but I didn't say anything. I didn't reply. I couldn't. I didn't know what to say.

"It's fine. But I have a question for you if you don't have a question for me. Would you be willing to answer me?" Hakeem sat back in his chair and crossed his legs again. He placed the book he held in his lap and locked his fingers together on top of it.

"Sure," I said with a fake sense of confidence.

"Are you a prisoner or a free man?" Hakeem asked me.

"I suppose I am free."

"A free man doesn't suppose his freedom. He isn't shackled by uncertainty and indecisiveness. A free man knows what he desires out of life. He knows who he is. And he surely knows if he is free or not. He does not suppose it. He knows it."

I paused. Baffled. This man schooled me so fast I could barely process what just happened. It was a truth bomb I was not prepared for. I had no armor, no shield, I had nothing. I managed to uncreatively respond with reciprocating the question.

"Are you a free man or a prisoner?" I asked him.

What may have seemed like an obvious question wasn't obvious to me. Well of course he is a prisoner you may say. He's serving time in a state penitentiary, unable to leave by his own resolve, dictated by the timetables of another authority. He's a prisoner. But I didn't feel it was that simple. A prisoner doesn't respond the way he did to my lack of certainty. A prisoner does not have that sort of intelligent eloquence, one not bound by a general prisoner's deficiency. Though that may seem like an unfair generalization that is at least how I honestly perceived the matter.

"Here, I am a free man, yet I live in prison. Outside of here, I was imprisoned by my freedom. I am a pioneer, an explorer in a cell shackled by his own past but freed by his repentance," Hakeem paused.

"You could say that I am a pioneer prisoner." He nodded in agreement with himself.

I was still fascinated.

"My father told me to come here." I blurted out.

"Do I know your father?" Hakeem asked intrigued.

"No, you don't. Well, he didn't specifically tell me to come here to visit you, or to come to this prison, or any prison for that matter," I explained.

Hakeem looked at me confused.

"What I mean is that my father told me when I was younger that if I wanted to be a man, I would have to ask myself a question. That question I don't think I can answer on my own. I thought you could help me."

"I like your father already," Hakeem smiled. "What was the question?"

I took a deep breath and continued.

"He said that if I want to be a man I should look at the struggles of others and ask myself if I could carry their burdens instead of my own."

"Did you answer the question?" Hakeem asked.

"No, I didn't."

"Well the answer is quite simple," Hakeem smiled again.

"What's the answer then?" I replied impatiently.

"The answer is 'I don't know'," said Hakeem.

"Huh?"

"What is the truth in this situation? Is it not that you don't know? Is it not that you really don't know if you could carry the burdens of your brother? Is it not that you don't know if you should assume you could? To presume either way would be doing an injustice to yourself and to him. You don't know enough about yourself and you don't know the struggles that he endures. You simply do not know, and that is half of wisdom... that is how you become a man."

I didn't need to ask Hakeem how his own personal experiences helped give him the wisdom that he articulated. I didn't need to be presumptuous and ask the obvious. I already did that. I listened and I got my answer. I looked around and found the beauty in his words in such a horrid place. How light can come from the darkest corners... I thought to myself.

"Time's up Hakeem," said another officer coming out from the observing room.

I got up and extended my hand out to Hakeem as I did in the beginning of our meeting.

"Thank you for giving me your time Hakeem, it means a lot to me."

"My pleasure young brother. Keep asking questions. Keep searching. Don't stop until you see."

"I will," I replied with a smile. I turned around and began walking for the exit.

"The unexamined life is not worth living..."

I looked back at Hakeem as he uttered those words.

"Socrates said that right before he was sentenced to death. He knew his living purpose until his dying moment."

I nodded and continued towards the exit.

5. THE SUMMER OF WAR

"I can get you on a flight two weeks from today for $1300. It's a roundtrip from here to Najaf, Iraq," the travel agent told me as she hammered away at her black keyboard situated on a small desk filled with paperwork and receipts.

Hadi and I sat down in front of her while Adam stood behind us leaning forward in between the two armchairs. "So, what's the route that we would be taking?" Hadi asked.

"You'll have a brief stop in London and then one night in Beirut. I can have you stay in Beirut for a few nights if you'd like. The cost won't change."

"Beirut?" I asked in disbelief.

The agent looked up at me not sure why I was asking about the transit with such surprise. "Uh, yeah," she replied slowly.

"I can take you through Istanbul or Doha but the prices are actually higher for the time you're looking to travel," she explained. "Is there a problem with Beirut?"

"Beirut will be just fine. Book it at three nights," Adam responded on my behalf. He saw that I was getting nervous. He grabbed my shoulder, looked at me, and smiled.

"It's going to be great," Adam reassured me.

I smiled back and nodded. The agent went on to process the paperwork for the tickets and take the rest of our information. Adam continued to speak on my behalf from that point forward because I basically checked out. My thoughts raced back to the images that will forever be in my mind, those of the last summer I spent in Lebanon – the Summer of War. That was ten years ago. It was as if in that small travel agency, I had already taken a flight back to Lebanon and found myself walking along Tyre's golden shores outlining miles of the Mediterranean Sea.

I looked up squinting at the clear skies that shined so brightly with its blazing sun. They say that the sun is millions of miles away, but I could swear that if I reached out to grab it I would melt away from its unforgiving heat. In any case, we didn't need the forgiveness of the sun when we jumped into the Mediterranean Sea.

The sun could chase after us all day and we wouldn't care. We would just dive off the boulder rocks that gloriously peered out from beneath the blue water at Jamal Beach in Tyre. On those boulders, we didn't have a care in the world. It never got old for us. We spent the whole summer on Jamal Beach. But this summer would be different. I was fourteen.

"All day, every day!"

Ahmad shouted out in his heavy accent as he jumped off one of the largest boulders into the deep waters in perfect cannonball form. His cannonball splashed us all even though we were a good five meters away. My friends and I laughed and teased Ahmad as we walked around like crabs, or monkeys depending on how you looked at it. I sat on one of the rocks for a minute to catch a breath and take in the scene. It was just so beautiful. We were having such a good time. Not a worry in the world. No screens in sight. No need to take pictures for Instagram or Snapchat, because they didn't exist. We took pictures with our eyes and savored the moments in our hearts and minds.

I looked towards the water and stared at it from the shoreline to the horizon. It was clear as day, so clean you could drink it. But of course, you couldn't really because it's salt water – the only downside to the mesmerizing Sea. I guess the Great Lakes had an upper hand here. I thought back to Mackinac Island and the few trips we took up there when we were back home. I mean here, Lebanon was home too, but you know what I mean. Well maybe you don't. Do you know what I mean? Do I know what I mean?

I drank the water on Mackinac Island without a single hesitation.

"What are you doing Ali?" Emily would shriek at me with a disgusted look on her face as I picked up the crystal clear water to my mouth.

"I'm drinking the best water this world has to offer. You look dehydrated, want some?" I extended my hand out to her.

"Ew! That's not sanitary. It hasn't been boiled or filtered or anything! You're going to get sick."

"Okay. Well maybe you can cool off then." I playfully threw the handful of water at her and it was on. Our match of water splashing went on for a good few minutes until we were both completely soaked. We laughed so hard it was difficult to breath. Mom and dad showed up after strolling behind us on their romantic walk and found us dripping wet on the rocky shore.

"Really Ali?" Mom said to me with her hands on her waist and eyebrow raised.

"She was dehydrated," I said with a shrug.

"I was." Emily nodded excitedly.

We looked at each other trying to hold back our laughter but it didn't last long. Mom tried to stay serious too but she couldn't help it.

"Hajj, I think our kids need some disciplining." Mom signaled at Dad with a nod of her head.

"It would be my pleasure *azizati*."

Before we knew it, Baba was slamming me back into the water, Mom jumping on Emily and falling into the water herself, and we were all soaking wet in laughter, gasping for air not because we were drowning but because how much we were laughing. Good times.

"What's that?" My lanky friend Zayn pointed out in the distance from the boulder rock we sat on as he stood to his feet.

"What's what?" Ahmad replied as he floated on the water below.

"That! Don't you guys see it?" Zayn pointed harder towards the western horizon thrusting his arm in full motion as if it would help us see what he was gesturing at better.

"No. What do you see?" Zayn's younger brother, Kamil, shoved past us, both standing up at this point, to get a better view.

I squinted hard and finally could make it out. My heart dropped.

"Those are ships. They're coming in this direction. But there is no port here," I said quietly. For a minute we all stood still. It was the longest minute I'd experienced. Frozen by the thought of what was to come we couldn't move. The voice of the groundskeeper behind us jolted us back into motion screaming at us to get out of the water in his southern Lebanese dialect.

"Ahmad get out of the water! We got to go!" Zayn called out to the floating Ahmad below.

"Why man? We are chilling."

"Ahmad! Let's go, come on!"

Ahmad grunted and moaned until he managed to get up to the boulder where we stood.

"I don't know why you guys are freaking out, it's probably just…"

Ahmad stopped mid-sentence and saw what we saw. Those were not ordinary sea-ships out in the distance. They were not friendly Lebanese ships. They were warships. Ahmad slowly turned away from his gaze upon

5. THE SUMMER OF WAR

the sea and looked at us. We nodded to him in acknowledgement of what we all saw and what was to come. We knew what we had to do and we knew we didn't have much time left. Away from the ships. Away from the Sea. Away from it all. We ran. We ran like we've never ran before.

The four of us sprinted down the Korneesh, or boardwalk, bustle and people looked at us like we were fleeing the scene of a bank robbery. Kamil yelled out as we ran passed swaths of people enjoying ice-cream and fruit cocktails,

"Bawarij Harbiyyeh!"

Warships. Kamil yelled out the word warships in Arabic. But people didn't flinch. Well at least I didn't see them flinch other than those we got so close to knocking down because of how fast we were running. Heck even Ahmad was keeping up with us at this point, which even with how tense the situation was I was still amusingly impressed by and couldn't help but chuckle. Zayn caught me smirking and yelled out,

"What the hell are you smiling about Ali?"

Mind you we are all running at full speed here and Kamil is still yelling out "Bawarij Harbiyyeh!" and people think we're crazy. Now Zayn thinks I'm crazy because I'm smirking as we run for our lives.

"I don't know Zayn I can't help it. Ahmad can barely pass his gym class but now he's running faster than me!"

Zayn couldn't help it either and burst into laughter. Ahmad was in the zone running down that Korneesh like a truck. I was sure glad I was running alongside him and not in his way, because if he ran into me I knew it would be lights out. No matter how built any of us got, by mere genetics Ahmad was always bigger. He was big-boned as they say. And Kamil kept at his viral announcement, "Warships! Bawarij Harbiyyeh!"

What finally got people's attention was the sound of fighter jets soaring above us. One. Two. Ten. That got people moving along. And before we knew it everyone was running. But the sweet thing about Tyre was it wasn't like the depictions of people in Hollywood block-buster films where they run frantically and sporadically all over the streets not knowing where to go or what to do. People knew what they had to do. How quickly they had to move. How much time they had and where exactly they had to run to. Even in such a gorgeous coastal city, in such a beautiful country, war was awfully too familiar. My parents always talked to me about their experiences growing up, both in Lebanon and Iraq, and how they had to run from fire and grenades. I did not know that I was about to experience my own war at the time, something that I could go on to tell my own children about one day.

We finally got to the main road away from the shore and spotted a taxi. I called out "Taxi! Taxi!" but to no avail. Zayn used his index finger and thumb, pressed them against his tongue, and let out a whistle that could be heard from a mile away. The taxi stopped and we had our ride.

"How'd you do that?" Kamil stopped and looked at his brother in amazement.

"Come on man! I'll teach you when we're not about to die!" Zayn hurried Kamil into the taxi, while Kamil had this big smile on his face looking forward to learning how to whistle like Zayn later on.

Zayn, Kamil, and I jumped in the back. Ahmad opened the front passenger door and sat next to the driver. Ahmad was the oldest, the biggest, and spoke the best Arabic out of all of us. All those factors lead to a lesser likelihood of us not getting clipped by the driver for an extra few thousand Liras.

"La wayn ya shabab?"

Where to boys? The driver asked.

"Nadi Al-Housh ya m'allim..." Ahmad began to reply calmly.

"Are you crazy?! Why are we going to the gym when there's warships out there?!" Kamil grabbed both headrests and thrusted himself forward and turned to the driver.

"Ammu, fi bawarij harbiyyeh bil bahr!" Uncle there's warships in the water!

The driver looked at Kamil with concern and replied, "I know, Ammu. Bes, where do I take you?"

"As I was saying, the house is right behind the gym. Remember?" Ahmad said as he looked at Kamil with eyes piercing embarrassment.

"Oh yeah." Kamil replied defeated. We pulled him back from the driver's breathing space and had him sit in between us. I put my arm around his shoulder and brought him in closer to me. Kamil was like the younger brother I didn't have. He was always so lively and rambunctious. Usually the youngest person in the room, he had such a way in making everyone laugh with his witty and dramatic sense of humor. At the same time the kid had spunk. Even though he was lanky with a small frame, he always held his own. That's why he was able to hang with older kids all the time.

I remember one time Zayn and I went to grab some sandwiches from one of our favorite spots, Abu Deeb Restaurant, while Kamil stayed outside to watch our bikes. We came outside to find him surrounded by three older guys that by mere virtue of height and size literally towered over him. As we got closer I could see Kamil's facial expressions and posture.

"I like your bike," the guy in the center said to Kamil with a smirk.

"They're on sale down the street," Kamil quickly responded coldly.

He only looked at the one guy in the center, the one who had seemed to be the leader of the crew. He looked him straight in the eyes, stood tall, shoulders back, and fists clenched. Little did they know that this bony kid was a black belt in martial arts, trained by one of the karate champions of Lebanon – Master Hicham Okasaki. He was half Lebanese and half Japanese, and by default the go-to expert on martial arts for anyone that was serious about the sport. Kamil was a whole lot of serious about it, being trained for six years at that point since the age of six.

"But I like this one and I think I'm going to take it," the guy said as he reached out for the metallic blue Schwinn, which was my bike. It's the one my dad had gotten me special ordered and sent to Lebanon to enjoy morning rides with my friends along the golden beaches of Tyre and in the banana orchards of the *Housh* right outside the city. I loved that bike. But I wasn't too concerned because Kamil was watching it. Before the big kid in front of Kamil could even feel the smooth metallic finish on that limited-edition Schwinn, Kamil karate chopped the guy's arm and pushed him back a few feet with the back of his hand. Talk about a boss. He was one.

I loved that kid.

On the short taxi ride home, we didn't talk much. Everyone was kind of in their own zone. Staring outside our windows, each floated in their own thoughts of what was ahead. The driver decided to break the cold silence with a question.

Looking at me through his mirror he said, "Where do you live?"

Ahmad turned to him and began to describe where the house was again by the gym.

"No. Where does *he* live?" Gesturing with his head to me. "He doesn't live in *Libnan*."

I was wondering what gave it away? Was it what I was wearing? My hairstyle? My accent? But I didn't even talk in front of him. Did I? I would later find out that taxi drivers, and most people in Lebanon for that matter, could sense if you were a "foreigner" even if you had Lebanese blood from both sides ten generations back.

"You live in Africa. No, actually no. Europe? Not quite." He was itching to find out where I was from but seemed to be asking himself rather than waiting for an answer from me. Then it hit him like a train and all the light bulbs in his head lit up.

"I know! You are *American*! Yes, you are an American. *Ma heik?*" He waited for his confirmation. But I didn't have to give it. He knew he was right. I just stared back in his mirror without giving a reply. Before it became awkward, Kamil leaped forward and said,

"Lak Ammu! My friend is one hundred percent *Libnani*, okay?!"

Kamil looked like he was about to karate chop this guy's head but thankfully the driver arrived at our destination, delivering us to the doorsteps of our 3-story apartment building nestled up against the back concrete walls of the neighborhood gym in the *Housh* suburb. I tipped him a couple extra thousand liras to smooth over any weird tension that we may have left behind and thanked him for the ride.

"Shukran Ammu," I said thank you.

He looked at the money I gave him, placed it in a small drawer in his middle console and said,

"*Amercani w nuss.*"

You're an American and a half.

He chuckled and drove off. I wasn't sure if that was because how much I tipped him or because I tipped him altogether. I forgot that people don't really give tips in Lebanon. So, in the end, according to our Lebanese driver, I guess I was more American than most. That wouldn't hold much weight in America though.

We ran up the stairs because the electricity was out. We had just missed the last hour of electricity for the day. It would be back on in another six hours. My aunt opened the door before we even knocked.

"*Waynkun?!* Where have you been? We've been worried sick!" She hurried us along inside where we found dozens of relatives, aunts, uncles, and cousins making their way to the family room through the large corridor of the grand three thousand square foot apartment. In the family room, the television set was turned on to the news. As the news broadcaster began his announcements the elders shushed everyone to a bleak silence that could hear a pin drop.

"We are reporting several towns and villages attacked by fighter jets near the nation's southern border." Images of bombs blasting, destruction, and people fleeing plastered our family room television as the news anchor detailed the scenes. For me everything went silent. I no longer heard his words. All I could see was the obliteration of villages that many people called home.

I looked around the room and found my aunts sobbing. The men were clenching their fists as they tried to console their wives. The children were wide-eyed, many of them never seeing anything like it before. It was like a new movie to them. Was it real? It couldn't be real. I watched as they processed and would soon have to register this as part of their reality.

"What is this?!" one of the uncles pointed at the television screen and yelled out.

"We can't just stand here and do nothing. This is our home," another uncle responded. I could see the fury in his watery eyes.

"What can we do? The army is barely responding to the attacks! If our army can't protect us, then who can?"

"You know who can and you know who will," the only uncle sitting down at this point said in a low voice. That was Uncle Moussa. Everyone called him *Khal*.

Khal lit up a cigarette and crossed his legs. He took a long puff from that Marlboro Light and exhaled a cloud of smoke that filled the room. Everyone waited to hear what he had to say. He was the *Khal*.

"Everyone has a role to play. But leave the fighting to the people that have already put their lives on the line to protect our homes and take back our land. You can criticize our army. You can criticize whoever you want. But in the end, young men will give their lives so that you can call this place home. Keep that in mind."

Khal took another puff of his cigarette. The room was still silent.

"This is going to be a destructive war. It may go on for weeks. It may go on for months. It's not going to stop at a few airstrikes. They're coming for Tyre. It won't be safe here for long. War knows no boundaries. It's a savage beast that will take women and children alike."

The women clenched on to their children and wouldn't let go, as if Khal's warning was about to take full effect within moments' time.

"So what are we going to do Khal?" one of the aunts impatiently burst out.

"We will get the families to safety tonight. We must move quickly. Only pack enough to put on your back or sit in your lap. We don't have much time. We will be going North or East. I'm waiting for a call for the green light. We should be on the road in an hour."

"East? Why East Khal?"

"Syria. It's the way out of the region. Beirut's airport will be shut down in a few hours. You'll see."

The aunts and uncles scattered to grab their things and prepare for the unplanned journey ahead. Khal sat back on the couch and continued smoking his cigarette. I walked up to the couch and sat next to him. He turned to me and patted my head.

"*Keefak ya Khal?*" He asked me how I was doing.

"I'm good Khal. How are you?"

He smiled.

"*Alhamdulillah ya Khal, alhamdulillah.*"

Praise be to God, he repeated in Arabic.

Khal's phone rang. He got up and walked out to the balcony to take the call.

Ahmad, Zayn, and Kamil came and sat next to me on the couch. I could tell they were scared. We all were.

"What do you think is going to happen?" Kamil asked the group but looking back at me as if I had an answer.

"You heard what the Khal said. Everything will be fine inshallah," I smiled at Kamil to reassure him.

"That's easy for you to say Ali. You're lucky you have another home in America. You have somewhere to go back to," Ahmad said to me in a defeated voice.

He was right. I did have another home to go back to. I was already thinking about how my family and I were going to get *back home*. But I didn't feel as if I was excluded from this tragedy. This was my home as much as anyone else's. That's how I felt.

"This is my home too Ahmad. I don't care if I have somewhere to go back to. I don't want to leave here."

"What if they destroy everything here Ali? What if we have nothing left? Where will we go? You're still American, you don't have to worry like we do."

Again, he was right. Their place here was different than mine. I was looked at as a mere visitor, a tourist even, with ties and roots. When it came down to it, I wasn't seen as one of them and I didn't blame them. They had so much more to lose. In the end, I still had America. *Home.*

The Khal would facilitate the departure of all our families from the South. We would leave late that night in about seven cars and trucks. There were about fifty of us, adults and kids, in total. The bombing had gotten even worse in those hours. Things escalated very quickly and those who considered staying and waiting out the ordeal were no longer keeping that option on the table. I overheard Khal talking on the phone with his contact about the distance the cars had to be from one another.

"They can't stay too close; it'll look like an envoy. That'll invite airstrikes." He spoke into his Nokia phone.

We all waited for his signal to go downstairs and take off in the cars. Each family was to stay together. We were mostly families of five to six people so it worked out well. In my case, my dad wasn't with us. He was back home in the States, so it was just me, Emily and Mom. He was worried sick. He kept calling my mom to check up on us. He even called the American Embassy in Beirut dozens of times to see what could be done to retrieve us from the war inflicted area. But to no avail.

I would later find out that the war affected him the most, even more than any of us. Being absent from your family during such a time can take a big toll on a father. My father was actually admitted into the hospital by my aunt while we were disconnected for a couple days from any type of phone service on the road leaving the South. My dad suffered from a heart attack but was strong enough to survive it and fully recover within weeks. We didn't find out until we got back to the States. Just the thought of anything happening to us and the fact that he could do nothing about it killed him. It actually almost did.

Khal arranged for our car to go to Syria while the other families would seek shelter in the North. There was a small town governed by a Christian friend of his. Though he wasn't officially elected, he was the defacto "mayor" of the town. He would open a few apartments, and even his own home, for our families to stay in while the South fell siege to the relentless airstrikes of the war.

Before leaving the South, however, Khal had to make a stop at the local hospital to see his friend who managed the place. It was the largest hospital in the South and the amount of injured and dead carried into the building from the bombings was excruciating. It wasn't the first time that I would see a dead body. I had witnessed the open casket funerals of both of my grandmothers, as well as other members of our family. But this was the first time I had seen women and children soaked in blood.

As I waited for Khal to come back to the car, I watched the ambulances race back and forth with bodies, some dead and some alive. One particular scene will never escape me. A father would jump out of his own car, pick up his daughter's lifeless body covered in blood from the backseat, and carry her into the hospital building screaming.

"Binti! Binti! Binti!"

My daughter. My daughter. My daughter. He repeated. That was the only word that he would say. A whisper. A scream. He was hysterical. I looked back at his car to see that his backseat door was still open. There was so much blood, it dripped from the edge of the leather seats down to the dusty hospital parking lot grounds. I could never forget that scene. The image of that little girl soft skin and light brown hair, soaked in blood, will be forever etched in my mind. Her name was Zahraa.

Khal hurried back to the car and we were on our way. Normally the drive would have taken us about an hour and a half. Because of the amount of destruction to the infrastructure of roads and bridges from the South outward, it took us almost four hours to get to the Syrian border. Craters, rubble, and impromptu detours were all we saw. We eventually arrived in Syria and would spend the night in Damascus. This was after four hours of driving and then another two and a half hours at the border. If Khal wasn't with us I don't know how we would have been able to make it. He made sure the other families were secured in the North with his friend, and he wouldn't allow my Mom and us to go on alone.

"You're my responsibility," he would tell my mom.

We spent the night in Damascus and I had the chance to visit the shrine of Lady Zaynab for the first time. Khal would take us all actually and we spent about two hours at the shrine that night. Emily and my mom would go in through the women's entrance and we wouldn't see them until we met back up at the agreed upon meeting place: Gate 3. Khal and I walked in through the men's entrance and grabbed us some prayer beads.

"Stay close and do as I do habibi," he told me as he wrapped his arm around my shoulders.

I went through all the motions with him. I watched his every move. I mimicked him until I understood the flow. That was the first hour. By the second hour I didn't have to glance at him. I had my own motion going. He knew what he was doing and I was following suit. Into the second hour, a large congregation was formed for a supplication. Since it was Thursday night I thought it would be for *Duaa Kumayl* – a supplication Imam Ali taught to his close companion, Kumayl ibn Ziyad. It wasn't to my surprise. As the supplication being recited, though beautiful, did sound unfamiliar to me, I decided to ask Khal about it.

"Khal, what supplication is this? It doesn't sound like Duaa Kumayl…"

Though Arabic wasn't my first language and my Arabic wasn't that strong, I still had a good sense of how the supplication flowed. This is, of course, being thanks to the many years of my childhood that my dad dragged me with him to the mosque on Thursday nights. The mere way that it sounded stuck with me as a kid and into adulthood. It wasn't something that I consciously learned as a young man; rather, it was wired through my nurturing as a child. All thanks to my parents, both for giving me greater consciousness and by making me look good in front of Khal for being that American kid who had a little bit more sophistication than most.

"It's actually *Al-Ziyaara Al-Jami'a*," he would tell me. I would later learn what great significance this particular supplication had. The Grand Visitation, it was called. It echoed the praises of the Prophet and his disciples, as the pathway to salvation and the grace of God.

Though I didn't understand much of what was being recited, I tried my best to listen. I caught words here and there and tried to hold on to them as much as I could. What I did hold on to most definitely was the image of Khal crying. His head was cradled between his knees and I could see him sobbing as the supplication was being recited. It was the first time I had seen him cry. A man with his strength and fortitude in crying as he prayed to God? That alone enfranchised me and moved me to tears. With the few words I understood, the image of Khal crying, and the dome of Lady Zaynab in front me, I experienced a spiritual high for a few moments. And even if it was short-lived, it was a full life experience in itself.

We had just escaped death. We could have been at the bottom of any one of those craters on our escape from the South. We could have been on one of those bridges that was struck by fighter jet missiles. We could have been killed in an airstrike that fell right outside the hospital we visited before we left – there were two of them that very same day. But we escaped death. Khal was our guide and his light surely shined bright.

When the supplication finished I watched Khal wipe away his tears with a black scarf he had wrapped around his neck. He wore that atop a black polo shirt and beige cargo pants. Khal got up to his feet and began scanning the wave of people around him.

"I'm right here Khal," I said only a few feet be-hind him.

He turned around and smiled. "Let's go habibi. You guys have a plane to catch tomorrow."

The next morning, we would fly out of Damas-cus and be on route home through Paris. Khal took care of everything and we were back home in the States within 24 hours of leaving Syria. When my father greeted us at the airport, he was beyond elated. I could tell he lost weight and looked like the time spent away from us aged him a few years. I was so happy to see him. But I could not escape the images plastered in my mind of the destruction and horror in the South. I couldn't help but think of my friends who I left behind. Though their families messaged us confirming they were safe and sound in the North, I still worried for them. I continued thinking about the war and the homes it destroyed. I could not escape the war in my mind because I finally knew what it was.

I didn't know what war was until I saw it with my own two eyes. I didn't know what it was until I saw a father holding his lifeless daughter in his arms, until he screamed her name and she didn't respond, until I saw her blood stain the dusty grounds in front of me. Her father couldn't accept that his pride and joy, his flower, the apple of his eye, his baby girl... was gone. She was only four.

I didn't know what war was until I lived through it, until I drove through the streets struck by missiles and saw bridges collapsed and craters instead of intersections. Destruction is not the same displayed through a television screen. I saw people's homes brought down to rubble. I saw mothers lose their sons and fathers lose their daughters. I saw families lose everything. I saw death. It was colorblind and indiscriminate. I saw war. It was unforgiving and relentless.

6. FLIGHTS WITH HADI

"I'm starving," Hadi growled as we watched the flight attendants painfully walk down the aisle with their measly food carts.

We were sitting at the very end of the plane. Row 48 to be exact. This was no ordinary ordeal. It felt like I hadn't eaten in days and Hadi wasn't any more patient than I was.

"How much longer do you think until the peasants in the back get some porridge?" Hadi said to the older woman wearing an embroidered brown hat with a small white feather on its side. Sitting to our left she smiled with her eyes wide open as if someone had been stretching her eyelids apart.

"Oh we're not peasants my dear and I'm sure they don't have porridge on this flight, that would be unbecoming of British Airways." It was the perfect candid commercial for the airline. I wish I had my phone out to record it but too bad it was tucked away in my hoodie pocket with my passport, boarding pass and chewing gum. Best of all though was that she had a British accent! Hadi turned to me smiling ear to ear like he couldn't believe it. This stuff happened to him all the time, why he was surprised beats me but I loved his youthful enthusiasm. It never got old.

Hadi went on to have this long candid conversation with, Mary her name was, about the history of British colonialism, the best types of tea, and the Queen of course. Anticipating the talkathon I plugged my headphones in and continued listening to an audio book I started at the beginning of the flight. I hated reading so I took up listening, I thought it would be a good compromise. My dad always told me to have a book in my hand and that anytime I didn't I was simply wasting my time.

"A good book is like good fruit. It has vitamins and nutrients that you'll only think about when you're older but then you are too old to enjoy the benefits. So eat your fruit young man." I like fruit. Books? Not so much. But hey I'm trying. The audio book I was listening to was called Difficult Conversations. I know I've had many of those, so I thought the books would be helpful. I didn't just stumble on the book though, it was a recommendation by a good friend of mine. A mentor actually. He recommends a lot of books but I rarely get to them. So reading, or listening, to this one is an achievement for me. Let's see how much I get out of it. It may be "life changing" he said. I'm not so sure, but what do I have to lose? I'm on this flight for seven hours anyway.

First stop. London. Second stop. Beirut. Final destination. Najaf. Yup. Hadi and I were going to Najaf, Iraq. We were going on Ziyara. I couldn't believe it. You may be thinking oh well that makes sense since your dad is Iraqi. You're visiting your father's home country and rediscovering your heritage. Some good deductive reasoning right there. Good on you mate! Wait. Or is it inductive reasoning here? I always mix the two up. Emily would know. Remember, she's the brighter one. Anyway, the reasoning you may or may not have come to is only partly true. You will realize, like I realized later on, that it goes much deeper than that. It wasn't merely learning about my father's homeland; it was learning about myself. I would end up learning a lot about Hadi too, but he's his own novel and at this point he's too busy talking about the Queen.

Our stop in London was only for a couple hours. Since we were in transit and I was pretty excited for our stop in Beirut before Najaf, I was actually glad we didn't have to stay in London long. Hadi was pretty bummed though. He and Mary hit it off so well, she invited him over to her home in London for biscuits and English tea.

"My lady, it would be an honor and a privilege," Hadi solemnly stated as he gazed intently into the regal woman's old eyes. It was getting weird. I nudged Hadi with my left elbow into his side. Startled he looked at me with fierce eyes I've never seen before. I switched to Arabic and said,

"Calm down. Stop being an animal. The plane is de-boarding. Let's go before I bury you."

The English translation seems a lot more intense than it actually is. I guess that's the effect of literal translations. I hate literal translations, so much meaning is lost. Or added. Anyway, Hadi caught a grip and broke his trance.

"I regret to say that the constraints of my travel schedule will not permit me the honor of visiting your auspicious residence. Though this is out of my hands and has been mostly due to the impatience of my travel companion, it is an unfortunate reality I must come to terms with at this time,"

Mary's smile slowly turned into a frown and her eyes watered. I was really starting to feel bad, but Hadi's poeticism was getting so good I wanted to laugh.

"Do not fright my dear. You will be in my thoughts and my prayers throughout my journey onward. I will visit you some day. If it is not in this world, it will surely be in the Heavens where you will ascend as one of its finest angels. I pray that I soar in the skies of such adornment alongside your angelic wings dear Mary," Hadi closed his eyes and smiled as if envisioning the scene he just painted with his words.

She still cried. But they were tears of joy. And as her tears fell I just had the urge to clap. But before I knew it, there was a standing ovation for this guy by all of the peasants of aisles 43 – 48. It was something you would see in a movie. And Mary was a class act.

"Be safe on your journey young man. And know that you always have a home in London."

Hadi nodded softly as she took the feather out of her hat and gently pinched it into Hadi's thick brown curly hair. She was so classy you would think she was related to the Queen. Hadi was just a goofball that enjoyed the sound of his own voice but he sure had these people thinking he was prince.

What was awesome is that the people in the aisles ahead of us waited for us to pass and cheered us on. It just got stranger and stranger to me. What happened when I fell asleep? What stories did Hadi tell this lady, and apparently this whole plane? No worries now, we had to get to our next flight. Beirut here we come.

We rushed past the aisles with our duffle bag straps crossed against our chests and a couple plastic bags filled with snacks from the Detroit airport. We took a sharp left, exiting from the plane and bid a quick farewell to the British Airways flight attendants that smiled radiantly and waved goodbye.

Because of the apparent delay and our oversight of the time change we only had forty minutes before our flight to Beirut took off. Hadi and I sprinted our way from the gate we arrived at in Terminal E to our gate of departure, Gate 45, in Terminal A.

"Let's go!" Hadi howled at me goofily as we ran past people dodging the unexpecting and oblivious. He flailed his arms up and down making light of the situation.

"Stop messing around Hadi. We're going to miss our flight!" I yelled at him as I trailed behind.

"Yeah because you're too slow!" he replied in laughter. Mocking me, he started running backwards. I had enough. I dug deeper, tied my strap tighter across my chest, and went in full throttle. I passed up my obnoxious travel buddy and saw his jaw drop as I flew by. I've never ran so fast before. I don't know what got into me. The spark of energy. The burst of fervor. Was it because Hadi was being obnoxious and calling me slow?

Or was it my fear that I was going to be delayed from my journey of enlightenment? I think it was both. Hadi was getting annoying.

"We're here!" Hadi shouted out to the flight agents at our gate. Luckily, we got there just as they were about to close the boarding doors. We searched our pockets for our boarding passes and passports and handed them over to the flight agent at the desk.

"One minute late and you would have missed this flight gentlemen," the agent told us with a smirk.

My hands were on my knees, and so were Hadi's. Well his hands were on his knees, not mine. Both of us trying to catch our breath, we couldn't even respond to her. All we did was look up and give each other a thumbs up. She chuckled.

"You're in seats 10A and 10B. Enjoy your flight to Beirut," she handed us our updated tickets.

"Looks like we got Economy Comfort Hadi," I said as I looked at the ticket.

"Oh yeah! That's what I'm talking about. No more peasant porridge for us. We're about the croissant and fancy cheese life now." Hadi twirled and did a Heisman move for some reason. I knew he didn't dance but it sure looked like he wanted to. I chuckled and heard the flight agent laugh some more as she saw us walk through the bridge. I guess she saw Hadi's twirling.

As we hurried through the jet bridge I asked Hadi, "What did you say on the plane so that all those people gave you a standing ovation?"

"What didn't I say is the more appropriate question," he replied smugly.

"Seriously Hadi. It was so bizarre and I can't remember if I fell asleep or what. What did you do?"

"Keep your eyes open on this trip champ, not a moment can be wasted or ignored," he winked at me and handed the flight attendant our tickets. She checked the stubs, smiled, and guided us to our seats. It was a breath of fresh air to see Mediterranean flight attendants. Don't get me wrong, I love the British but it was a sense of home that I got on this flight to Beirut. That even if I was late, I was still welcome. Maybe I am reading too much into it but that was my feeling as I walked unto that plane. Kind eyes and bright smiles to the tardy millennials. It felt good.

We sat back in our seats and sighed in relief. We made it. "You didn't think I could run that fast did you?" I turned to my left and said to Hadi with a smug smile on my face.

"You didn't think you could run that fast either big guy," he responded with a wink. Hadi reached down into his bag and grabbed a book and began reading from a used paperback publication. He went from complete goofball to wisely absorbed intellectual. Though I knew Hadi when we were kids I never really *knew* him. So much of this trip was learning about him, how he behaved, and how he thought. He definitely was an interesting character. Full of life and energy, yet deep in thought and contemplation. How the two were so integrated and encompassed in one body simultaneously was beyond me.

"What are you reading?" I asked nosily.

"The Alchemist," he replied without having his eyes leave the words he read.

"What's it about?" I continued.

He looked up at me, closing the book on the finger he used as his bookmark. "You haven't read The Alchemist?" Hadi asked surprised.

"No, I haven't. Relax." I replied.

"Just pulling your leg champ. It's about a kid who goes on a journey and meets an alchemist. He shares with him life's secrets. The end." He held back his laugh with a straight face.

"Seriously?"

"I'll let you read it in a bit, I'm finishing up the last chapter," he said and returned to the book.

Frustrated I said, "Why don't you just tell me what the stupid book is about?"

"First of all, calm down. Second of all, it's not stupid. Third of all, what the hell are you going to learn in life if you're just told what it's about in the end? You have to put some work in."

Unsatisfied with his answer, I looked away and began fiddling with the TV screen in the headrest in front of me. I flipped through the selection of movies for a few minutes and before I knew it Hadi placed the book in front of me.

"It's all yours."

I handed it back to him. "I'm good. I'll just watch a movie. Thanks."

I didn't want to be childish but Hadi had a way of getting under my skin.

"Just read the first few pages," he replied.

"Hadi I told you…"

"Trust me," he interrupted and handed it back to me.

I took the book from him and began to shuffle through it. I started reading. I got through the first few pages. I continued. I finished the first chapter and decided to keep going. Before I knew it I was finishing the book and the plane was about to land. For about four hours I did not move anything except my fingers that turned those pages.

"That was amazing!" I turned to Hadi as I completed the book with tears in my eyes. To my luck, the kid was knocked out with his head cocked back against his head rest and his mouth wide open. I took a picture of the scene. It was priceless. Am I mean for that? Absolutely not. I needed the ammo, because I am sure Hadi will get in at least a few pictures of me snoring and drooling during this trip. Nonetheless, I fell in love with that book. It was as if it told a story that I was searching for. As if Hadi planned to bring that book with him just so I could ask about it and eventually read it. As if...

As if Hadi was going to stay asleep any longer. Yeah right. The guy woke up and started talking before his eyes opened.

"I told you you'd like the book," he smiled.

I punched him in his shoulder and chuckled.

"You ready for our stop in Lebanon?" he asked as he rubbed his shoulder.

"I sure am!" I said excited. "I haven't been here since the War." I paused solemnly.

"Wow," Hadi replied. "Well, things have definitely changed since then brother."

"How so?" I asked concerned.

"In a good way. A lot more construction. Places are cleaner now. Some cities even have traffic lights!"

"No way!" I replied.

"Yeah!" Hadi was just as excited as I was. I loved this guy.

I started bouncing up and down like a schoolboy on a field trip. I missed Lebanon. I didn't realize how much I missed it until I saw its shorelines as we descended into the Beirut airport. I plastered my face to the window and watched the waves crash against that Mediterranean shore. I admired the coastal construction and gazed outward into the mountainous east. How so many landscapes and terrains could be combined in such a small area of God's Earth always boggled my mind. That was the beauty of Lebanon.

But things can often be so beautiful from a distance and yet so surprisingly different as you come closer. Not that it isn't beautiful up close, but the beauty you expected from a distance wasn't what you were greeted with when you came near.

The few days that we spent in my mother's homeland were enjoyable. I reconnected with my childhood friends Ahmad, Zayn, and Kamil. They really liked my friend Hadi and we all had some great laughs over a late night dinner at the beach. Though it had been years since I've seen them, it felt like it was just yesterday that we were diving off the Jamal Beach boulders into the Mediterranean Sea.

Outside of that though, Lebanon wasn't the same as I remember it. Things did change as Hadi said, but not all for the better. I don't know what it was exactly. I couldn't tell. Maybe we weren't there long enough. But what I did feel was a sense of superficiality I didn't feel before. Maybe I didn't sense it because I was younger then? I don't know. When I was younger, though, I sensed a spirituality and a connection that went deeper than what I intuited during this brief trip. Maybe my purity had faded and my intuition was lacking? Maybe the flaw was in me and not the atmosphere I walked through? I don't know. All I know is it wasn't the same.

Those three days seemed shorter than three hours. We had gone down to the South for two nights and spent the last night in Beirut before taking our flight to the holy city of Najaf. Departing from Lebanon was a breeze. We got to the airport two hours early and were basically the first ones there for our flight. We went through security and walked to our gate. Beirut's airport is not big at all so there's only so many places to roam around to kill the time. Instead of roaming, we decided to just chill at the gate area.

I didn't feel the excitement I thought I was going to feel. Instead, I had a stomach wrenching nervousness that I couldn't seem to wean off. The fact that we got there so early wasn't helping either. I crossed my arms across my chest and rocked back and forth for a while. Hadi had gotten up to grab us something to drink and was gone for a good twenty minutes. When he came back, he saw me in that position.

"Hey, bud. What's going on? Why you look so pale?" Hadi said with a southern accent.

"I'm good." I replied without looking up at him.

"You're nervous. Don't be." He said nonchalant-ly.

"It's that simple, huh?" I responded mockingly.

"Yeah it is. You choose to speak. You choose to rock back and forth like an obsessed nutcase. Choice is yours. Choose to be calm and cool."

"I'll be fine." I kept at my rocking business until Hadi came up behind me and started massaging my shoulders.

"Hadi. What are you doing?" I said uncomfortably.

"I'm trying to get you to relax."

"Okay, thank you. But please stop." I replied looking around to see who was watching.

"Not until you're relaxed," he said as he continued to rub my shoulders.

"Bro! There's people around. Stop it." I said under my breath.

"I won't stop until you're calm and cool."

I threw his hands off and sat up straight. "I'm calm and cool. I'm calm and cool."

"Excellent!" Hadi replied with a big smile and sat down next to me.

"Jesus..." I murmured.

"Hey! Don't use the prophet's name in vain." Hadi glared at me.

I chuckled. He was right though. It still made me laugh. I'm telling you this guy was a character.

We boarded the plane and were airborne within twenty minutes. The flight crew announced that the projected airtime was just shy of an hour and a half. It was like a drive from Detroit to Lansing. How awesome is that? I thought to myself, "Why didn't people fly from Beirut to Najaf more often?" It wasn't expensive and it was so short. Turns out more and more people did. In fact, I would learn from Hadi that a sizable population of Lebanese students were actually studying in the Islamic Seminary in Najaf. That tidbit didn't make up for the weird feeling I had while I was there though. It was hard to shake off. What would make up for the void I felt was the fulfillment of seeing the Shrine later on that night. Though it would be my first time, it was as if I had longed for it deep in my soul. As if I had lived there before and yearned to return. Maybe in a life before this...

7. MY FATHER'S HOMELAND

We arrived in Najaf. The humbleness of the airport was befitting of what I expected of the city. Small, quaint, and nothing fancy. I liked it already. What did hit me was the heat. Oh boy was it hot. They didn't have a jet bridge like most of our airports in the States. Instead, you got off the plane using a staircase that led you to sizzling asphalt. From there, you walk over with your carryon luggage to a bus about twenty feet away. The bus drives you to the entrance of your gate at the airport building. The two minutes between walking down those steps and to that transport bus, reminded me of the days I worked at my friend's pizzeria. It was perfectly reminiscent of the moments I opened the stone pizza oven and rotated the pizzas while my face was exposed to its scorching heat. Yup, that's what it felt like — a pizza oven. No matter how hot it got, I loved pizza. So just like the pizzeria, I would get used to Najaf's heat.

"Isn't it great?!" Hadi would exclaim embracing the air.

"What's great?" I said with my eyes squinted from the dry heat and scorching sun of the afternoon's clear sky.

"The heat. It's purifying. Let your sins melt away with this beautiful Najafi heat…" Hadi closed his eyes, tilted his head up towards the sky and smiled.

"You're nuts," I said. I couldn't wait to get in that air conditioned bus. I'll melt away my sins when I shower and put another stick of deodorant on. Believe it or not, those two minutes drained me so bad, I felt more tired in those moments than the combined traveling of all the flights we took here since leaving the States.

Hadi had a friend of his waiting for us at the passport counter that worked at the airport. He got us through customs and security without a hiccup and we were in a car and on our way to the old city within twenty-five minutes. VIP treatment right there. Ten points for Hadi.

"*Masaakumallah bil kheir*," the driver greeted us with the traditional Iraqi greeting. It's the equivalent of the Lebanese *masaa' elkheir*, or the English *good evening*. Hadi appropriately replied, "Allah bil kheir aghati," in perfect Iraqi dialect. He wasn't even Iraqi! Show off.

It seemed like the driver knew Hadi from his previous trips and didn't need to ask where we were staying. Instructions were already given and arrangements already made. I was looking forward to observing the road action on our way, but as soon as we hit the highway I fell asleep. What I do remember was seeing a few motorcycles with open back flat beds bustling through traffic. Some carried fruits and vegetables and others carried people. Multi-purpose. I wish we had some of those back in the States. Who needs an F-150 when you can drive a *Sattoota!* That's what they were called in Iraq. In fact, a lot of young guys made a living by driving Sattootas and transporting goods, or people for that matter. Hybrid taxis maybe?

Hadi woke me up when we got to our building. It wasn't too long of a drive, half hour tops. It was a much needed power nap though. Hadi paid the driver, gave his salaams, and we grabbed our bags from the trunk. The driver insisted on helping us but Hadi insisted that our luggage was minimal and light. Appreciation was exchanged and we went on our way through the building entrance.

We walked up four flights of stairs because the electricity was cut off. Nothing new to me, I was used to it from our visits to Lebanon as a kid. One summer, we were staying in an apartment building that was 12 stories high. We were living on the 11th floor. So whenever the electricity cut off, which was several times during the day, we would have to take the stairs. That summer I could have sworn I lost a good fifteen pounds. If only that was the summer after my freshman year of college.

As Hadi got settled in our room, I decided to walk around the building and check the place out. Let's just say the amenities were not so plentiful. I went out to the rooftop and saw the rows of laundry hung to dry. I thought it would be cool to explore the laundry maze and see what else was on this Najaf rooftop. I felt like a voyager on a mission. What are you trying to find? I thought to myself. The missing towel? Haha. I crack myself up. But my humor was interrupted.

"Can I help you sir?" said a voice from behind me.

I turned around and found a young man, about eighteen years old I guessed, standing there waiting to help me. He spoke English and his accent sounded Indian, so I assumed that's where he was from. India, Pakistan, somewhere in South Asia based on his facial features, skin color, and accent.

"Oh, no thank you. I'm just walking around. I just got here." I replied and gave him a thumbs up. What was that I immediately thought to myself? Why did I give him a thumbs up? I can be so awkward sometimes.

"Okay sir. You are very welcome." He smiled and walked off disappearing in the ocean of white laundry. I instantly thought of the legendary magician Houdini. Was Houdini an Indian name? I know that the magician himself was white, but why did he have an Indian sounding name? Wait. Maybe it's just me and it really doesn't sound Indian. The thoughts boggled my mind as the young Indian man vanished in the laundry maze. I would later do some research to find out that Houdini, Harry Houdini to be exact, renamed himself following the last name of a French magician he admired named Jean Eugene Robert-Houdin. Turns out the name is French. Go figure.

When I walked back to our room I found Hadi waiting for me at the door of the room. He raised his phone towards the ceiling searching for a signal.

"Can't get connected?" I asked.

"It's fine. Just need to stretch out sometimes you know." At this point he was standing on the tiptoes of his left foot fully extending his right arm to the nearest corner of the hallway.

"Yeah, stretch it out brother," I chuckled.

"Got it!" He jumped up in excitement.

"We're meeting the *Sayyid* in twenty minutes. He just confirmed," he said looking down at his cellphone.

"Oh cool." I wasn't expecting that we would see him so soon. We had just arrived. But I was excited to meet him. "What should I wear?" I asked Hadi.

"Clean underwear." He replied.

"Really?"

"Wear whatever you want. Come on, we're late already," he responded sassily.

I gave him an annoyed look, walked past him and quickly put on a pair of slacks and a button up shirt laying on my bed. My father always told me that if I was ever unsure of what to wear, I would be safer to dress up instead of down. "Dress up or dress down? You never go down baba. You always go up."

So I went up. Thank God I went up. I would later find out that the expected attire in the city, and the country generally, was dress clothes or a *dashdasha* – a traditional long one-piece robe. Most people wore white or black, though earth tones were also very common. Your option was traditional or formal attire. Scrubbing out wasn't looked upon favorably, especially if you were Iraqi.

"So where are we meeting him?" I asked Hadi as we walked down the flight of stairs.

"He invited us over his house for dinner," Hadi replied with a big smile. I could tell he was excited for the meal. Either the Sayyid's family made some good food or Hadi was just really hungry. Or both. It was both.

Apparently the Sayyid's house was not too far from where we were staying. Obviously, Hadi led the way and I'm glad he did. He really knew the place. To me, it kind of looked like the laundry maze I witnessed on the rooftop of our building. But here it was a maze of brick, concrete, and clay construction. Some were homes, others were small apartment buildings, and others were shops and offices. Electricity lines crisscrossed above us as we walked through the alleys of the neighborhood. Right. Left. Another left. Right again. And within a few minutes we were there. Hadi was Lebanese, but after that walk I felt like he was definitely more Iraqi than me.

On the way there, Hadi gave me a brief breakdown of who the Sayyid was. I knew he was a scholar and a professor in the Islamic Seminary. However, I didn't know much beyond those generic titles. Hadi gave me a decent overview so that I knew who I was about to meet and eventually spend most of my time with during my Ziyara journey.

"The Sayyid is one of the top scholars in the Islamic Seminary after the first layer of *Maraje'* – the grand religious jurists. In knowledge and studies, he is counted amongst the elite. What sets this guy apart though is two additional things. For one, he is humble beyond imagination. Some think he is even too humble for a man of his knowledge and stature. I would say it's the secret to his success. Secondly, the Sayyid is the grandson of one of Najaf's grandest scholars and mystics..."

"Mystics?" I interrupted inquisitively.

"Yes. Don't misunderstand what that means. It's basically a person who is extremely spiritual and understands what spirituality is. None of that pseudo fake bull crap that some people are feeding us nowadays. It is actual spirituality based in the teachings of our Prophet and his family. This Sayyid was raised in such a household. Some say that he follows so closely in his grandfather's footsteps that almost every aspect of him resembles the late *Marja*."

"His grandfather was a Marja too?"

"Yup."

"Why is someone like *me* meeting with *him*?" I asked doubting my qualification to be in the presence of someone with such a lofty status. Who am I? I thought.

Hadi smiled. "Because you may very well share that same secret to success."

We arrived at the quaint home with a concrete wall that surrounded the small property, adjoined with neighboring homes. A large grey metal gate was the entrance, upon which Hadi knocked on twice. Not too lightly but not too hard either. A young man, I figured the Sayyid's son, opened the door and greeted us with a big smile.

"Salaamu Alaykum! Hadi!" he embraced Hadi with a bear like grip. Hadi squeezed back. It seemed like they've known each other for years. He then looked towards me and his smile brightened even further.

"Salaam! You must be the Ali we've been waiting to meet!" before I knew it he was embracing me as well. A hug and a kiss to the shoulder is what he gave me and I already felt like I was a part of the family.

"Come in, please come in! The Sayyid is waiting for you and so is dinner," he chuckled hurrying us along past the gate and into their humble home. We took our shoes off in the foyer and walked down a hallway that led to a large living room. The home was bare. White walls. A mix of tiles and commercial carpet between the hallways and rooms. As we entered the living room, I looked for couches, sofas, or chairs, but found none.

Seating was on the floor. Plain navy colored cushions outlined the edges of the room, between the floors and the walls. And there the Sayyid was. Sitting down on the floor with his back slightly supported by the wall behind him, and his books stacked around him like a fortress. Through his old school oval glasses, he read from a book propped on his left knee and took notes on a small note-pad with his right hand. What humbled me even further is the fact that when he noticed us enter by way of the old squeaky door, he would rise from his study, put the books to the side and greet us with open arms.

"*Ahlan ahlan ahlan*," the Sayyid repeated 'welcome' with his deep raspy voice as he got up from the floor to welcome us. The Sayyid struck me as tall and handsome, especially for one who is fifty-seven years old. If it were not for his greyed beard, his tight fair skin and round green eyes would have you fooled for someone in his forties.

"Asalaamu alaykum Sayyidna," Hadi would say as he embraced the Sayyid and kissed him on his shoulder.

"Wa alaykum asalaam *ibni*," the Sayyid responded. He called him *ibni*. My son. I wasn't sure if that was a general greeting of endearment or it was special for Hadi. After his brief exchange with Hadi, I stepped towards the Sayyid and he turned to me.

"Asalaamu alaykum Sayyid," I said as I kneeled in for a hug and a peck to the shoulder. I tried to mimic Hadi's movements as closely as possible so that I was sure I was doing things right.

"Wa alaykum asalaam! Ahlan wa sahlan bil Hajji Ali," he replied to me during our brief embrace. Hajji? I wasn't a Hajj. Did he think I was a Hajj? I really hope I don't disappoint him because I'm not a Hajj, I thought to myself. Turns out people in the Seminary, and in religious circles generally, address non-Sayyids and non-Sheikhs as Hajj or Hajji.

"Please sit. You've had a long a journey. You must be exhausted. Sit down," the Sayyid gestured with his hands towards the cushioned floors. *Ga'da 'Arabiya.* Arabian furnishing. That's what it was called. We sat down on the modest floor-level furniture and I found it to be surprisingly comfortable. It wasn't my first time sitting on one of these sets before. I experienced it once before in Lebanon, at my mother's uncle's house. It was a tad fancier but the whole setting just wasn't as common anymore.

"I'm sure you are hungry," the Sayyid said to us looking back and forth between Hadi and I. Honestly, we were starving. But we had to remain cordial and respectful. We both smiled and didn't reply affirmatively or negatively.

"How are you Sayyidna? *Mishtaqeen*," Hadi said to the Sayyid. We miss you.

"Alhamdulillah. Nahnu alashwaq ibni," the Sayyid replied. We miss you more my son.

Before the pleasantries could continue, the Sayyid's son reentered the room with a supersized round metal tray carrying what seemed like a five-course meal. He placed a disposable table-cloth, or floor-cloth in this instance, in front of us. He then went on to situate the many dishes of food between us. There was qoozi rice and lamb, chicken drumsticks over another set of rice, bamia (okra) stew, Iraqi kabobs, Arabic salad, lentil soup, hummus, roasted egg-plant, and some other things I'm sure, but I was so hungry I couldn't keep count. There was a lot of food, but at the same time we had some deep appetites that night. We chowed down. Thankfully the Sayyid was a spirited fellow and he didn't mind our informal approach to the meal.

After a few minutes of chowing down, the beautiful setup the Sayyid's son orchestrated now looked like a murder scene. We plucked those drumsticks dry. Qoozi? What qoozi? The only thing that remained were a few lumps of white rice. Without a moment to spare, then came down the tea. Oh and what tea this was. I am not a tea drinker. But from that moment on, all I wanted to drink was tea in Iraq. Sayyid's son served us tea in small traditional glass tea cups. The tea was black, not merely black leafed, but nearly black in its color. Iraqis drank their tea very dark. What compensated for the strong black tea was the fact that they also drank their tea very sweet. So the black tea was accompanied by a tablespoon, not a teaspoon, of sugar. I was dozing off after dinner but with a sip of that traditional Iraqi tea, I wanted to bounce off the walls.

"Have you visited the shrine since you've arrived?" the Sayyid asked us as he sipped on his cup of tea.

"No Sayyidna, we haven't had the chance to yet. We were planning on going later on tonight after seeing you," Hadi replied.

"If that is your plan then we can go together if that's something you gentlemen would like," the Sayyid responded.

After dinner and tea, the Sayyid normally would take a walk through the neighborhood and head to the shrine to give his nightly salutations to the Commander of the Faithful, and kneel before God in prayer. He considered changing his plans for us since we were visiting him. But since we hadn't gone to the shrine yet either, we would all go together. I was geeked. At the same time, I was nervous about going. Maybe the mixture of high emotions was due to the massive sugar intake I just had with that tea. Was I having sugar with my tea, or tea with my sugar? Whatever. It was great.

As I walked along the edges of the narrow alley-way with the Sayyid I looked at the ground and did not say much, I didn't say anything at all. He was dressed in an impeccably clean white dashdasha that seems so straight it must have been ironed for hours. At the very least, it wasn't ironed by the laundry crew where I was staying that's for sure.

"You don't speak much," the Sayyid said to me as he looked on to the remainder of the alleyway ahead while counting his prayer beads in one hand.

His statement made me flinch and evidently un-glued my eyes from the old brick pavement. Hadi chuckled to himself. I think he enjoyed seeing me get nervous. All part of the experience I guess.

"My apologies Sayyid," I replied nervously.

"There's no need to be sorry, son. I would just like to hear you speak."

I nodded but didn't say anything. What do I say? What if I say something wrong? I don't want to look like a fool in front of this scholar. Disgrace myself and my whole family. So I rolled the dice and stayed silent.

A few more moments passed. Silence.

The Sayyid scratched his beard, turns to me again and said, "The Commander of the Faithful used to say, 'Whoever speaks increasingly also increases his chances of making mistakes.' It's a good rule to live by and I appreciate your application." The Sayyid paused and looked away. He smiled and turned to me once more, "But now, I don't want you to worry about what mistakes you can make. Speak. I want to hear your thoughts... even if it's only one thought."

That made me even more nervous. Just share one thought. You can't even share one thought? I had to say something, otherwise it was just going to get unbearably awkward and I was going to look incompetent. So, in my broken Arabic I managed to ask Sayyid the following question.

"Sayyid, do you think America is a good place for us to live as Muslims?"

I wasn't sure if the question was good or bad. It felt like it was a hit or miss. But the Sayyid smiled and he nodded his head. He caressed his grey beard and gave a few "hmms".

The Sayyid began speaking to me about opportunity in America and the great deal of it that exists for all people. It was honestly bizarre that a person who I assumed would be so immersed in Eastern culture was so optimistic about what America, the posterchild of the West, had to offer the world. But more specifically what it had to offer Muslims.

"There is a real opportunity for young people in the United States to make a difference in their lives and the lives of others. Your country is an open playing field for anyone that wishes to take on the challenge and seize the day. The system itself is up for grabs merely by the way it was constructed. At the same time, the American culture is always in a state of hunger. If you have people with the patience and endurance that are willing to feed it, they can dictate whether to feed it what's healthy and nutritious or whatever they desire to intoxicate it with…

"America's people are passionate and driven. They are hungry for success and results. But the lack of direction in American culture can be alarming. She, America, wants to achieve something in this life but she's not sure what it is or how to get to it. She is ambitious, hungry to get things done, but for what exactly? She's not sure.

"Her passion and ambition attract people from all over the world. In her essence, she embraces everyone and allows space for you to grow somewhere in her vast land. In fact, the whole world follows her, because she is steering the ship. And she will steer it for the long haul because she has the drive and endurance for the task. The questions is… where is she going?"

I never looked at America as a woman before. Well I never really thought about it as a man or a woman quite frankly. The Sayyid's analysis was almost poetic. It personified the nation and it made a lot of sense. I couldn't believe a non-American could open up eyes to America in so few sentences as the Sayyid did in those moments. He did make me think of the Statue of Liberty because of how much he referred to the country as "she". She, Lady Liberty, is the first "she" that came to mind.

The Sayyid placed his hand on my shoulder and intently slowed our pace a bit. I looked over to him. His face was still facing straight ahead.

"Beyond a discussion of America and your place there, I want you to know something very early on son." He placed his hands behind his back and continued to fiddle with his prayer beads.

"You have a place wherever you go in this world. All of it, the four corners of this world, all of it is God's Earth. You can roam it as you please, so long as you re-spect it and those on it."

I nodded my head in acknowledgment. My mind automatically began racing with different images of places that I have studied throughout history. India, China, Russia, Brazil, Mongolia, Panama, Angola, South Africa. There were too many to name.

"But you should definitely know that it is important for you to be here. Fate brought you to your father's homeland. And by father I do not mean your biological father. I am speaking about our father, the Father of the Orphans, the Prince of the Believers, the Commander of the Faithful. Imam Ali ibn Abi Talib. Fate invited you here, you accepted the invitation."

The Sayyid patted me on the shoulder again, like a welcoming embrace to the invitation that I had accepted. I looked at him and smiled. He made me feel welcomed. He made me feel safe. He made me… happy.

We were nearing the shrine. We could see it now from the beginning of the street we turned on, Al-Rasool Street. I could see its golden dome from a distance as we got closer. It was mesmerizing. I felt as if it were pulling me closer and closer to it. Gravitating. I am here. I am actually here. But what was here? What was I visiting? Whose home did I enter?

The Sayyid raised his hand towards the shrine as we walked closer and closer, sending his salutations. *"Asalaamu alayka ya mawlay ya Ameeril Mu'mineen,"* he would say repeatedly. *Peace be upon you, my master, the*

Commander of the Faithful. I saw Hadi do something similar but couldn't make out the words he repeated.

While the Sayyid indulged in his salutations, and Hadi in his prayers, I had time to reflect on the questions I was just asking myself. Who is this man that is pulling me towards his shrine? In what place am I that I feel such ease, yet I have never been here before in my life? What is it about this place that makes me feel... home?

I thought that what I would remember would be the books I had read in the couple weeks prior to my trip. I took Adam's advice and decided to read some books about Imam Ali so that I could be a bit more sophisticated as I visited his shrine. I deepened my knowledge base of history and what Imam Ali meant to his admirers and enemies alike. In fact, there was a recurring theme that I noticed. Ali was admired by everyone. No matter how much people disliked him, they were still in awe of his unwavering commitment to God and his Prophet. Even his staunchest enemies could not hold themselves back from admiring and respecting him.

I read that Imam Ali was the Prophet Muhammad's champion and rightfully so. He was his right hand, ever since he was a child. He was actually raised by the Prophet himself, Ali's first-cousin. He was the son of Abu Talib, the Prophet's uncle. Not only was his upbringing unique, being raised in the cradle of revelation, but his birth was miraculous. When his mother Fatima bint Asad was going into labor, she happened to be at the site of the Kaaba. As the pangs of child birth overcame her, the walls of the Kaaba cracked open allowing for a walkway for her to enter. She would walk inside, guided by angels, and give birth to the most beautiful baby boy the world had seen. The only individual in history honored with being born in the Kaaba itself was Ali ibn Abi Talib. He was so close to the Prophet Muhammad, that many described him as the Prophet's *shadow*. He would grow up to be the Prophet's confidant, disciple, and successor.

One particular story that I liked was about how the Prophet escaped an assassination attempt thanks to Imam Ali. The situation in Mecca had gotten bad as the people of Quraysh were fed up with Muhammad's "new religion". They wanted to get rid of him. The Prophet became aware of the threat to his life and that on one particular night there was a plan to have him killed during his sleep in his home in Mecca. The Prophet asked Imam Ali if he were willing to take his place while the Prophet would slip through the darkness of the night and escape to a new destination, Medina. To the Prophet's proposition, Ali would smile and go into prostration. As his forehead rubbed the ground he would say, *"Alshukru lillah. Alshukru lillah. Alshukru lillah."*

Thanks be to God.

He thanked God for the opportunity to lay his life on the line once again, as this wasn't the first or last time, for the Holy Prophet. I was so moved from that story, and the many other stories I read about his life and inspiration. I benefitted tremendously from those books that Adam told me to read. However, the stories and principles provided in the pages of those books were not what popped in my head as I walked towards the golden dome of his immaculate shrine.

What came to my mind were brief moments and memories from my family, lodged way back in my sub-conscious. What came to my mind were my mother, my father, and Emily. What came to my mind were people that I loved so much, who loved me even more, and who attributed their ability to love because of the man whose shrine I walked towards.

I remembered how each time my father got up to go to work in the morning, he would jump out of bed saying the words *"Ya Ali!"* Those words he would repeat when he started his car and drove to work. They would echo again when he came back home from his long day; as he would lift me off my feet, toss me in the air, and catch me as I grew in laughter.

I remembered my mother dressing in black and mourning every year for a few days, a little after the midway mark of the month of Ramadan. As a kid, I asked her why she was sad. She would look at me with a half-broken smile, touch my face with her soft hands and say, "I'm remembering who you were named after habibi."

I thought of how no matter how upset my parents were with me when I did wrong, they were always calmed by saying my name. I didn't understand it as a child. But simply saying my name, not because it was my own but rather for whom they named me after, they were put at ease. I remembered my father. I remembered my mother. They engrained in me an attachment to a man I thought I knew nothing of, but really, I had known my whole life.

Before entering, I read the poetic supplication hung over the doors of the shrine. In Arabic, it would read…

I, your servant and the son of your servant,

have come to you seeking your refuge,

bringing myself to your shrine,

turning my face toward your place,

and begging Almighty God in your name…

May I enter, O master?

May I enter, O Commander of the Faithful?

May I enter, O proof of God?

May I enter, O trustee of God?

May I enter, O angels of God who reside in this shrine?

O master, may you permit me to enter

in the best way you have ever permitted any of your devotees?

If I am too little to deserve such permission,

then You are too exalted to deprive me

I was not deprived. I was not denied. God's grace encompassed me as I entered. I sought permission and I was granted. A rush of emotion purged through a river of tears from my eyes. I saw visitor after visitor throw themselves onto the silver enclosing that housed the grave of the Imam. Hundreds of people pressed up against each other crying, wailing, praying, supplicating, whispering, and calling out one name... Ali. I've never felt closer to my name and yet so detached from my own self when hearing it. I called that name too. Without feeling I began calling out, not my name, but his. Ali. I approached the enclosure of the grave and couldn't hold myself back from latching on to it. I grabbed on and let my tears flow. Why was I crying? I truly did not know. But my tears overcame me and I couldn't hold them back. I didn't want to hold them back. It felt right. And even though I latched on and embraced the shrine, it felt as if the shrine was embracing me.

8. I DON'T NEED RELIGION

I was told that anywhere I go in the Middle East, I should bargain. So I applied that rule as I walked the streets of Najaf as well. Generally, I fared well. I think. At the very least I managed to get a price down from where we started, even if it were only a couple thousand dinars. One particular store wasn't the same though.

I walked up to a shop that sold almost exclusively *masabih*, prayer beads. I thought to get some as gifts for my Mama, Baba, Emily and Adam. As I examined some of the masabih that hung from metallic hooks, I asked the shopkeeper, "How much for these?"

"They're as much as you would like," he replied without hesitation.

I smiled politely and asked again, "I'd like five of these. How much would they be if I get five?"

He smiled back and repeated, "They're as much as you would like."

It was getting a little frustrating. But I thought, you know what, if he wants to play that game I could too. So, I grabbed those five masabih and placed them on the glass counter in front of me.

"Okay. I'll take them all for five thousand dinars," I said with a straight face.

He smiled, put the items in a gift bag and placed the bag in front of me. "Here you go," he said.

"You're going to take five thousand dinars for these?" I asked in surprise. Was he calling my bluff?

"That is how much you would like to pay, isn't it?" he asked.

"Yes, yes it is," I replied unsure of myself.

"Then that is how much you will pay," he smiled again.

I paused, looking at him trying to understand why he was doing what he was doing. I mean how does this guy make money if he just tells every customer to pay as much as they please? I knew for certain that each one of those masabih was at least five thousand dinars, and I was about to walk away paying only a fraction of the price. What was going on here?

"Why are you doing this?" I asked the man. "Why don't you just charge me? It's your right."

His smile was unwavering. "I do not like to negotiate my sustenance with someone who is delivering it to me."

"What do you mean?" I asked confused.

"My sustenance isn't from you, it's from God. But even though it's not from you, it is still through you, whether I like it or not. So, I won't argue with the messenger since it's no use. What God has given me will get to me." He grabbed the bag and handed it to me. "So pay as much as you would like." He smiled.

Inspired. Confused. Happy. That's what I felt from that brief exchange with the shopkeeper, all at the same time. I didn't give him five thousand dinars. I ended up giving him fifty. Maybe that was his way of getting the customer to pay more? I fought the urge to delve deeper into cynicism. But even if it were so, that is a pretty impressive way to make a profit with inspiration and class. More power to you shopkeeper.

That night the Sayyid told me to meet him at Baab Al-Saa'a or the "Gate of the Clock". That would become my favorite entrance to the holy shrine. When you walked in, you were just overcome by the grandeur of the golden gates of the shrine. I had never seen a sight so beautiful. I took a few steps inside and found a nice spot near the entrance alongside a humble bookcase of copies of the Holy Quran and supplication books, mainly *Mafatih Al-Jinan*. I took my seat and looked up at the shrine. From the dome to the minarets and the entrance to the tomb itself, it was overpowering. I could have sat there for hours. Turns out I did.

"There you are," I heard the familiar voice from my right.

"*Salaam Sayyid*," I turned and said as the Sayyid walked up and sat next to me.

"*Wa Alaykum Asalaam*," said the Sayyid as he slowly sat down with his hands holding his knees. I had to scoot a few inches to the left to make room for the both of us. He seemed tired. I guess a long day of teaching and studying. I learned that he was always reading or sharing what he had read over the years with his students. There was never a minute wasted with him. So I'm sure he appreciated that minute to just sit down and relax before the grandiosity of the immaculate shrine. It was a bit crowded there that night. But I couldn't hear a sound.

"I don't need religion." I said to the Sayyid as we sat down gazing at the golden Shrine of Imam Ali. He slowly turned to me. I could see him from my peripheries. He was squinting his eyes at me as if I was suddenly blurred to him and he was trying to see the soundness of my statement. His head slightly tilted.

"If you don't need religion, what do you need then?" he asked inquisitively.

I looked on at the golden gates of the shrine, I couldn't keep my eyes off them. They fascinated me ever since I set eyes on them. How can a shrine be so grand yet so humble? I had never seen gold to be such a gateway to one's spiritual heart like I did when I gazed at that shrine. It captivated me like nothing I have ever seen before. "Him. All I need is him."

The Sayyid smirked and looked back at the shrine. "Seems to me that you're confused son."

"What do you mean?" I asked with my eyes still fixated where they had been for minutes.

"How can you claim to need something and not need it at the same time?"

I now turned back to the Sayyid.

"He is religion." He said softly.

My eyes grew wider as if they were the gateways to soul. I felt his words deep within me like I hadn't felt words so true before. *He is religion.* It echoed in my mind again and again.

But I had more in my mind about religion. Even if it was as perfect as I see in the greatest student of the

Prophet, practically what role does it play in my life? I wanted to know how it works, how it should work...

And per usual the Sayyid basically read my mind.

"Look around you. This world is an amazing place. Humanity has been able to accomplish so much throughout its time in this world. We have used the faculties God blessed us with to build civilizations, expand empires, and explore lands unknown. Today, skyscrapers touch the clouds, technology connects people from across the globe, and man has gone to the moon and back.

"So what role does religion play in all of this? Can religion claim these breakthroughs experienced by humanity? Is religion responsible for these sort of advances and discoveries? Should we even expect religion to bring forth these forms of accomplishments? Not at all.

"You see humanity builds the structures with all of its resources. Science, technology, and whatever else is at the disposal of man is used to construct, build, explore, and establish. The possibilities are endless. Let's say we constructed the building. Foundation and skeleton is solid. Material is poured. The building is up. You see it. But something is missing. Is it paint? Decorative stone or bricks? Framing for the windows and doors? What do you call these?"

"Finishing touches?" I added.

"Exactly! Finishing touches." The Sayyid patted me on the back excited that I had completed his thought. Though I almost coughed up a rib as he patted me, I was really humbled. A man of his caliber in knowledge was appreciative that I helped him find the words to describe his thoughts. That stuck with me.

"Religion is responsible for that. The finishing touches. Religion is not supposed to replace science and technology, it has come to complete it. Religion is the artistic element, the flavor, the pizzazz!" There was no real Arabic equivalent of the word "pizzazz", and I have no idea how he pulled that word. So, it goes without saying that stuck with me too.

"So it's like that thing that people felt like they didn't have before and when they have it they realize what they were losing out on."

"You're catching on." He smiled.

I paused. "So we need religion and without it we're astray, lost, and vulnerable? But what about the other things that make us happy and complete? You can't just be spiritual; you need other things too? Right?" I asked realizing my thoughts weren't as organized as I would have like them, but Sayyid didn't mind that. He could cipher through. He knew what I was trying to say.

"Of course. Firstly, spirituality or being religious and materialism are not mutually exclusive. Think about it like sugar to coffee. They mix with one another and give you the taste you need. Not too bold and not too sweet. Just right." The Sayyid then took a sip out of a white foam cup of coffee. Where did that come from?

"It's like meat and poultry… you say the required prayer during the slaughtering process with all its prerequisites and it becomes permissible. Without that one word, it's not. It's a material that lacks the spiritual element to be complete for your consumption.

"Secondly, and more importantly, do not let anyone tell you that we as human beings are sick," the Sayyid asserted. I was taken aback by the firmness of his statement. I listened on.

"Religion is not a pill for the ill. We are not ill. We are not diseased. We are the ambassadors of God and we are capable of amazing things. Religion comes to help us perfect our amazing work. It organizes us and helps us put things in perspective. It's psychology not psychiatry. It's a matter of facilitation, organization, and formation…"

I nodded my head satisfied with these answers, so satisfied I felt like it opened a few roadblocks in my mind regarding faith. Within moments, a bearded man in a white turban walks up to where we were sitting looking at the Sayyid with a smile. I noticed him in periphery while Sayyid continued to gaze on at the shrine.

"Salaamu alaykum Sayyidna," the man says to the Sayyid and kneels to greet him. Caught off guard, the Sayyid turns to him and was pleasantly surprised.

"Mashallah! Wa alaykum asalaam Sheikhna!" the Sayyid replied as he tightly embraced the Sheikh. Turns out the Sheikh is an old friend of the Sayyid's who he hadn't seen in over twelve years. They were colleagues in the Islamic Seminary in Qum, Iran during the eighties. The Sayyid, along with many other scholars and students in Najaf, were forced to flee Iraq due to the persecution of the Baathist regime. Some seminarians did stay, but many left fearing for their lives and the lives of their families. With the toppling of the Baathist regime in 2003, many of them returned back to their homes in Najaf and continued their lives of teaching and scholarship there once again.

The Sayyid and the Sheikh switched back and forth from Arabic to Farsi, so I didn't catch the whole conversation. Studying in Iran, seminary students had to pick up the language as it was part of the seminary curriculum. As the language of the country, courses were mostly taught in Farsi, not Arabic. What I did catch from their multi-lingual conversation was that they were extremely happy to see each other, the Sheikh was visiting for a couple weeks, and that the Sayyid invited him over for a late-night dinner. The Sheikh apparently didn't want to impose, but the Sayyid insisted. I sat there quietly admiring the genuine exchange between old friends. The Sayyid finally turned to me and before he introduced me I got up and gave my *Salaams* to the Sheikh.

"This is my friend and my son, Hajj Ali. He is a bright student of history, visiting us from America," the Sayyid said as he patted me on the back. I was humbled by his introduction. I mean he didn't have to introduce me at all, I've been in those situations before. Don't you hate when that happens? You're a mutual contact but are easily ignored or forgotten by your friend. Well the Sayyid didn't forget. He never did.

"Mashallah! How are you brother Ali? My name is Ali too. It is a pleasure to meet you," the Sheikh responded in English actually. He did have a heavy Iranian accent, but I was definitely appreciative nonetheless.

"I'm great, alhamdulillah, how are you Sheikh?" I replied with a big smile.

"Bah bah bah bah! You're speaking English now? Are you soon going to apply for American citizenship too?" The Sayyid nudged the Sheikh. They both laughed and took a few jabs at each other in Farsi. I need to learn Farsi.

After the jabs and jokes, I followed the Sayyid and the Sheikh in prayer and supplication in the shrine. The Sheikh recited a supplication as he sat between the Sayyid and I. The Sheikh had a beautiful mountain-man type voice. His voice was so strong yet angelic in a way. It put me at such great ease and was truly one of the most endearing moments of my life. Sitting in that shrine next to these two honorable scholars, and listening to the Sheikh recite. It took me back to my visit to the shrine of Lady Zaynab with Khal. In those moments, I cried. For so many different reasons, I cried. Particularly for a verse the Sheikh recited in that supplication that struck a chord with me.

And I, O my Lord, am seeking refuge with Your benevolence

As I am running away from You only back to You…

I thought of the many moments of dishonesty I had with myself. The many times I doubted my faith. The times I felt angry and frustrated with the world. In all of it, I knew what was right but would divert my path because of the overwhelming feeling of instability within. I ran away. Ultimately from God. But I couldn't escape him. I couldn't flee from him. Because any which way I would turn, He was there. Any path I wished to take, He created. Anything I wanted to use, was His. That verse recited in the Sheikh's mountainous voice was like a revelation for me from the Heavens. The Sheikh would never know how grateful I was for him, he had no idea.

The Sheikh would come to the Sayyid's home at about 9pm for the late dinner. The Sayyid would invite some other colleagues, scholars of the seminary, as well. Hadi helped the Sayyid's son with the arrangements and getting the food prepared. I ran a couple errands to the nearby minimarket. Bottled water, Kleenex, and a box of Mars chocolate. That apparently was the Sheikh's favorite. One after another the scholars came in to the Sayyid's living room. I shook each of their hands and said Salaam. One particular scholar shook my hand longer than the others.

"Wa alaykum asalaam, Ali." He knew my name. I was humbled but still weirded out by it. Not creeped out, but it just felt strange. In some way, I kind of felt like I should have known him as well. His name was Sheikh Haidar Al-Najafi. I smiled and looked away. I felt like it was rude to continue looking someone in the eyes for too long. He patted me on the shoulder and continued towards the rest of the congregation.

Dinner was served. Between take-out and some home-made dishes, Hadi and the Sayyid's son really pulled it off. It was great. Maybe even better than the dinner we had the first night we got there. The tea then came down immediately after while we quickly cleaned up. The tea was a necessity for any gathering, especially after food. Not having tea was like not wearing clothes. You didn't have to think about it, it was a natural and necessary part of your day.

With the tea at play, discussions quickly ensued between the scholars. There were about ten of them in total including Sheikh Ali and the Sayyid. I sat and observed the scene as they went back and forth. Somehow the conversation took more of a political twist, examining the position of Iraq in today's geopolitical climate against a historical backdrop.

I noticed that the Sayyid doesn't like those type of discussions and quickly changed the subject. It was Sheikh Haidar who seemed to be the most interested in it. Turns out he studied history at the University of Baghdad, in addition to his seminary studies. Go figure.

After the gathering, I approached Sheikh Haidar and asked him, "What do you think are the greatest achievements for Iraqis as a nation? In the past century particularly. I'm not talking about the seminary or Najaf. Outside of that…"

Sheikh Haidar smiled as he adjusted his turban. "I'm guessing you studied history in the university like I did, huh?"

"Yes. Yes, I did." I replied excitedly.

"As students of history, we often neglect personalizing what we study. And if we do personalize it, we pick and choose. It can strip us from our identity or strengthen it," the Sheikh began. "Don't let history change you. Embrace it. Be normal. Don't be someone you are not because you may disapprove of something in it. Live your normal life. Be you."

I wasn't expecting such an introduction; still, I was pleasantly surprised by it and continued to listen attentively.

The Sheikh continued. "Never be ashamed of where you came from. Why are you scared or hesitant to show your roots? Of course, when society has a favorable view of a certain group then it is easier for us to identify with that part of our identity. But what about when society doesn't hold you in such a high esteem? What if the world is looking at you like an outcast? A heathen? An abomination? What then?

"What's the reason for it? Perhaps it is due to the failures of others. Take our great religion of Islam for example. Today Islam is seen as the face of failure in the world. Why? Anytime you hear about terrorism on the world-stage, it is almost always associated with the religion. Right?"

He waited for my reply. I thought it was rhetorical.

"Yes," I quickly said.

"The same goes for many countries of Islamic origin. Iraq. Iran. Egypt. Afghanistan. That is then associated with a person's citizenship and national identity. A person doesn't feel a sense of pride in their religion or home countries anymore. Let's not go too far out, take yourself as an example of this."

"Me?" I replied in surprise.

"Yes, you. You definitely identify as an American, don't you?" This one was rhetorical, he didn't wait for an answer on this one. "But after that, you will identify with your mother's home of Lebanon before you identify with your father's home of Iraq. Put aside your Americanism for a minute. You are more Lebanese than you are Iraqi. Why?"

I paused. I didn't know what to say because I never thought about this before in such a way.

"Because you don't feel a sense of pride in Iraq. You see it as a failed nation. And that is the root of your question. You don't see achievement in Iraq, you only see failure. Being American intensifies that for you, but keep it aside. You see Iraq as an utter failure. But you're terribly wrong and naïve for that. You don't know what Iraq is nor does your father."

"Excuse me?!" I was deeply offended that he brought my father into this discussion in such a way.

"Finally, he speaks! This whole night we haven't heard a word from you. Speak your mind!" He shot back at me.

I didn't hold back. He wanted me to speak. I'll speak. "My father left Iraq because it was nothing but hunger, tyranny, and oppression. There was nothing for him here. He went to Lebanon and eventually America because he had to. He had no other choice. He escaped a dying country and he survived. He latched on to life. He is a survivor and he knows very well what he did."

"But it is in Iraq where life started my son. It is in these lands that your father's skill for survival was harvested. Iraq is a part of his identity, his strength, his being a man. He doesn't speak to you much of it because he fears you are too gentle to know the truths he experienced. So it appears as dismay. In reality, it is mere protectiveness. You're a product of a different culture and a different time. All he has ever tried to do is protect you. I only said that to rile you up to talk. I know your father well. He knows Iraq more than I do." The Sheikh smiled.

"You know my father?"

"Yes. I knew him and your late uncle. Your uncle was a student of mine long ago, before he was martyred in the revolution."

"Wait. What? Revolution? My uncle?"

"Maybe we should sit back down."

I sat back down without taking my eyes off Sheikh Haidar. My uncle was in a revolution? In Iraq? The Sheikh and I would sit down for another hour or so talking about the rise of rebellions in the South and the North against the Baathist regime. It was in February of 1991, that Iraq's Shia and Kurdish populations mobilized to overthrow Saddam Hussein in what was called the Sha'ban Intifada. My father had left Iraq in the eighties before the rebellions took place. But his younger brother, Muhsen, stayed behind and continued studying in the Islamic Seminary of Najaf, withstanding the persecution and political pressure at the time. Sheikh Haidar was one of his teachers. He described him as tall, articulate, humble, and sharp in analysis.

"He was one of my favorite students. He was probably one of the youngest amongst them too," the Sheikh added as he reminisced.

During the Intifada, from the North to the South, the whole country was up in arms against the Baathist dictatorship. Even the scholars of the Seminary took part in it, which was generally uncommon given the Seminary's quietist approach to political affairs historically. The leading Marja of the time Grand Ayatollah Sayyid Abulqassim Alkhoei quietly authorized much of the movement. His house was described as a *mu'askar* – a barracks – for the revolutionaries. Sheikh Haidar and his students, amongst those who also stayed in Najaf during the turmoil of the eighties, would heed to the call of God and Country. They would partake in the revolution. My uncle would be killed in a gun fight with Baathist soldiers, along with some of his colleagues. Sheikh Haidar survived with gun wounds tracing his right arm and shoulder towards his back. I saw the scars. I was quickly reminded of the wounds I witnessed in Lebanon during the Summer of War.

"I was the one who delivered the news to your father when your uncle was killed," Sheikh Haidar said with his head down. "It devastated him. He always wanted Muhsen to leave Iraq with him. He understood why he wanted to stay, but he loved him so much. They were very good to each other."

It was coming together. My father's fear for our safety was not merely that of a father for his children, incapable of coming to their aid. It was coupled with his sense of failure to rescue his younger brother. My father never did talk about uncle Muhsen. All I knew was that "Uncle Muhsen died at a young age back in Iraq." He did die before I was born but I guess I know why it would pain my father so much to go any further than that.

"Be proud of your roots. Be proud of your heritage Ali. Your uncle died protecting his religion and his country. Your father survived to give you and your family a better life, so that you could come back and discover this great pride. You come from a family of scholars, fighters, and survivors. Don't forget that."

I couldn't hold back my tears. I was overwhelmed with emotion. I hugged the Sheikh tightly and sobbed for a minute on his shoulder. He embraced me and rubbed my back. It was calming but I couldn't stop crying. I eventually did though and thanked the Sheikh for sharing what he shared with me.

"You have so much Ali. Not just here or there. Everywhere. You have so much." Sheikh Haidar said with a smile.

"Thank you Sheikhna, I really appreciate everything you shared with me." I replied wiping away my tears.

"Give my regards to your father, he is a great man."

"Of course."

Before leaving, Sheikh Haidar turned around and looked at the Sayyid who was on the other side of the living room reading one of his books. The Sayyid gave him a smile and nod of approval, Sheikh Haidar smiled back, placed his hand on his chest for farewell and walked out.

Hadi and I went back to our place shortly after. On our walk home I was mostly silent. I was filled with just so many thoughts and emotions, it was hard to talk. Hadi would break my silence with a statement like I've never heard.

"You suppose you are insignificant, while within you lies the greater universe…"

I turned to him to find him smiling as he looked back at me. Those weren't ordinary words of wisdom, the source had to be something divine. The inquiry spoke to me like revelation.

"Where did you get that from?" I asked Hadi inquisitively.

"The one and only," he said as he nodded his head in the direction of Imam Ali's shrine.

I continued to repeat those words in my mind. They spoke to the deepest part of my soul. Could it be? Within me?

The greater universe...

9. LAUNDRY ON THE ROOFTOP

I followed the young Indian man through the lines of laundry on the rooftop of the 4-story building we were staying at in the old city. He was wearing blue jeans and a flannel patterned short-sleeved shirt. His clothes were visibly worn down, but he looked neat and tidy. He walked quickly so I had to keep up. I ducked through scores of undershirts, pants, underwear and *dashdashas*.

He handed me my bag of cleaned clothes. I looked down into my bag and could visibly detect that the clothes were still wrinkled. Back in the States, that would have warranted a nice complaint and a discount. But I wasn't in the States and everything here was already discounted. We were paying pennies on the dollar for food, taxis, laundry, and pretty much everything. So I brought the bag closer to my face, took a whiff of the newly cleaned bag of clothing and thought to myself, "Hey, they're not perfect but they do smell nice."

I gave the kid a couple thousand dinars, smiled, and went back to my room. I had a white dashdasha hanging, having been perfectly ironed the night before from the shop that I bought it from. "What the heck?" I thought to myself. I put it on, looked in the mirror, and said, "Not bad Al, not bad." Yeah, I actually said that out loud.

The Sayyid told me that he would be in our area and he would meet me outside our building for one of our nightly walks. As I walked down the steps arriving at the last flight of stairs, I could see the Sayyid through the glass door entrance. He stood there looking up at the sky as if he were searching for something. And in his right hand he held his *masbaha*, counting his prayer beads as his lips moved ever so lightly in a continuous fashion.

As we walked along the Sayyid didn't say much. So, I naturally reciprocated. The silence was shattered with a question he asked me after taking a good look at what I was wearing.

"Do you feel more religious when you are dressed like that?" The Sayyid asked me as I fixed the scarf upon my shoulders that I laid atop of my flowing white dashdasha.

"What do you mean?"

"How do you feel when you're wearing a pair of jeans versus wearing the dashdasha? Does the dashdasha make you feel more religious?"

"I suppose it does, yes." I replied cautiously. It actually did make me feel more religious. I thought that, yes, it felt like I was dressing the part.

"So you feel like you're dressing the part?" he replied.

No way. Is he reading my mind or something? I thought to myself. I just stayed silent and nodded slowly. It was an uncomforting feeling that I barely knew him, but he knew me so well. Was I that easy to read?

"Don't worry you're not the only one," he reassured me. I still felt like he was reading my mind. "The dashdasha is traditional Arab clothing. Being religious isn't equivalent with being Arab. It doesn't mean being Eastern for that matter either," he explained.

"Should I not wear this then?" I asked, doubting myself and my authenticity at that point. I mean I was of Arab descent, but my Americanism reigned in the eyes of any native Arab.

The Sayyid chuckled. "No habibi, keep your dashdasha on we're in the middle of the street." He patted me on the back.

I smiled painfully and turned red in the face out of embarrassment.

The Sayyid noticed my blushing. "I'm not saying this to discomfort you. It's to the opposite effect. I want you to know that you don't have to change your identity in order to practice. If you are comfortable in your dashdasha as part of your Arab roots, excellent, wear the dashdasha. And wear it with pride! You should be proud of your heritage and where your family comes from. You should never be ashamed of your past or where you come from."

I was confused. Should I wear the damn dashdasha or not?

Puzzled I began to say, "So…"

"So should you wear the dashdasha or not? You feel like you're getting a mixed message here right?"

"Yes Sayyid. I'm sorry I guess I'm just not understanding."

"There's nothing to be sorry about. I've only given you half of the picture. And with half of the picture you only have half of the truth. The other half is just as important and even more important when you have both."

"Yes, of course." I said trying to stay intellectually involved and not look like an idiot.

"You should be proud of who you are. Every part of who you are. You are an Arab and an American. That's your heritage and your citizenship. At the same time, you are a Muslim, which guides your worldview on how you see your Arabism and your Americanism altogether. You cannot neglect any aspect of your identity. Because each one of them helps make up the person that you are. This is without considering your own unique experiences, thoughts, and ideas that you hold as an individual."

This was getting deep and was making more sense. But when was a conversation with Sayyid not deep? I mean even over a cone of ice cream he got me questioning my life's purpose.

"Keep it natural is what I am saying, son. We all need to be real with ourselves. We are who we are. Let's own up to who we are and face reality. Don't be a person who puts on makeup, beautifying him or herself, keeping it on for so long and then forgetting to wash your face for days or weeks. You'll wake up one morning and realize that you haven't washed your face in so long. But when you do, and you wipe away all that beauty supply, you won't see much beauty at all. Not because you aren't beautiful. But because you've gotten so used to the façade you created that you don't recognize who you see in the mirror."

Woah.

"Your beauty is in you no matter what background you have and where you come from. Your religiosity and dedication to your values and beliefs comes from that same principle. Your idea of religiosity should not be based on a shallow beautification of image; it should be founded in your behavior. Modesty is not seen merely in clothing, it's in your walk, in your speech, in your gaze and in your thoughts. It's a full package. And you can be that full package as you are, whoever you are. Come from America, Indonesia, Pakistan or Iraq. Come as you are, whoever you are. Be religious, observant of your obligations, conscientious of the rights of others, and you will be just fine."

"I'm keeping the dashdasha on Sayyid," I said confidently.

He laughed. "Yes, please keep it on."

"But I'll probably put jeans back on when I leave back to the States, don't you think?" I cracked back.

"You in jeans and me in slacks."

We both laughed.

"Sayyid, I often think about how we believe in something we don't see. It's not that I don't believe in God or the Prophet or the Imam. It's more so how do I have a relationship with something, or someone, I can't see. It just seems so hard." I thought out loud. The Sayyid apparently liked the raw question though.

"It is hard. No one said it would be easy. But is it natural? Most definitely. Is it the only relationship you can't see with your naked eye? Absolutely not."

"What do you mean? How does that work?" I asked inquisitively.

"Can you build a relationship over the internet? Can a blind man love his wife without seeing her face? Can a deaf woman love her husband without hearing his voice?"

I thought about those questions and was getting ready to answer, but Sayyid continued on before I could reply. I guess it was merely rhetorical.

"There is a story about a woman who was severely burned from a fire that destroyed her home while she slept. Her husband was away for work. In surviving the fire and destruction, she endured terrible burns that disfigured much of her face and her body. Not possessing the same physical beauty she once had, she quickly fell into a depressive state. Why? She was convinced that her husband would not be able to love her anymore because how she looked after the fire. 'How could he love me when I looked like this?' she thought to herself as she gazed at her reflection in the mirror.

Her husband returned from his work trip but also came back with news of alarming change. Towards the end of his trip, her husband curiously lost his sight. He went blind. He would come home, embrace his wife, and tell her how much he loved her. They lived together for forty years in love and harmony, before she passed away. His love was not dependent on his sight. He loved her blindly. He loved her with his heart of hearts."

"Wow. Is that a true story?" I asked so moved by it.

"I am honestly not sure," the Sayyid chuckled. I laughed too.

"A monkey in his mother's eye is a gazelle," the Sayyid said. "That's a true story!"

We both laughed harder.

"But of course don't limit your understanding of the God's love by these physical temporal examples. They are just meant to bring the idea closer to us." The Sayyid said as I nodded my head.

"You see, love transcends time, matter, and space. We would be limiting love if it is merely based on the senses. Love knows no limit. If love can be experienced in such a way between human beings, how do we explain our relationship with God? It is existential, it is human, it is innately a part of us.

"Love, and all of its synonyms – we don't want to get into all the technical differences between the words – is a human thing. It's not merely about beauty or what catches the eye. If you see a beautiful woman, what happens to you? You get infatuated. Let's say you gather the courage to go forward to speak to her and introduce yourself. She gazes at you and you gaze back. But as soon as she spoke, all of that beauty went away…"

"She was an angel until she opened her mouth," I interrupted.

"Yes. Exactly! Did you just think of that?" the Sayyid asked with some excitement.

"No, it's an American phrase."

"You could have fooled me and just said yes."

"I could never fool you Sayyid," I replied.

The Sayyid smiled and nodded slowly. "Her beauty is limited by sight. When you are not looking with your eyes, but rather with your soul, your love sees no limitation."

"That makes sense," I replied.

"Do not love with your eyes, Ali. Love with your soul. You will see a lot in life. It's mostly a façade. Don't be fooled by infatuation. Love with your soul."

Love with your soul.

When we entered the shrine that night, I thought about people in my life that I loved. Mama. Baba. Emily. Adam. I loved them. I could soon add Hadi and the Sayyid to that list. I prayed for each of them that night and gifted a prayer to each of them by name. I thought that would be special. They treated me like family, or better, and expected nothing in return. Wasn't that love? To give and not expect anything in return? I would suppose selflessness is essential then. Imagine if you are to care for someone without expectation, and they were to care for you without expectation, wouldn't everyone be taken care of? Goals.

The Sayyid's use of the term "infatuated" during the discussion on the way to the shrine that night struck me. I know I have had my fair share of being infatuated. I thought back to the times I thought I was "in love" and the struggles I faced throughout high school and college in identifying relationships and trying to do things right. I went through a phase of wanting to try new things and not being too concerned about the immediate or long-term consequences of my actions. At the same time, I wasn't crazy. I didn't go out and party. I didn't go clubbing every weekend. I wasn't about that scene. I'm not saying I didn't make the mistake and curiously check those places out either. I wish I never had though.

"No matter what I tell you, you're going to choose your own path in life. When you fail and when you fall, don't stay down there for too long. Pick yourself back up and move forward. Don't lay in the dirt," my father told me after I graduated from high school. I took his advice. Surely, I did fall. Surely, I did fail. But I didn't lay in the dirt.

During my sophomore year in college I talked to this girl in my class. Rima was her name. She was a tall, thin, fair skinned brunette with a spunky attitude. She was semi-religious and semi-cultural. By that I mean she wouldn't "date" but she had no problem with us "talking". So we talked. And talked. And talked some more. We were talking all the time. Texting. Calling. Facetiming. All the time. Several months of talking got out of hand. By that I mean there was a lot of emotion involved without much intimacy.

What two naïve kids thought to be "love" was nothing more than a really bad headache. I was infatuated. She got attention. We tried to be respectful by not doing what couples do. We didn't go out alone, we didn't go on "dates", because again we weren't dating we were just talking. At the same time, we couldn't "talk" to other people. There was a possessiveness on both of our ends. We were reserved for each other in a sense. Saving ourselves for each other, for a future marriage that was nowhere reasonably in sight for our nineteen-year-old selves. The combination of emotion and ambiguity only added frustration and caused us to argue and bicker. The more we talked the more we argued. After about seven months of this "relationship", I was fed up. During one of our talkathons, I asked her over the phone.

"Are we married?"

She laughed. "Last that I checked there's no ring on my finger."

"And you're not my fiancé, right?"

"Again, no ring, no thing."

"So, are you my girlfriend?"

"Of course not Ali. You know that. I'm not that kind of girl." She replied sharply.

"So are we just friends?"

"You look at us as just being friends Ali?" she responded offended.

"No, I don't. I'm trying to figure that out."

"Why are you asking these questions anyway?"

"I'm trying to understand how the hell two people can spend so much time together, bicker all the time, and yet can't even define what kind of relationship they have."

She went silent.

"We're talking." She broke her silence and said.

"About what? We talked and talked and talked. What the hell are we still talking about Rima?!"

"Are you breaking up with me?"

"No! Because there's nothing to break up!"

She started crying. I heard her whimpering over the phone even though she tried to conceal it.

"Come on. Don't cry please."

"Why are you being so mean to me? What did I ever do to you?"

"I'm sorry. Don't cry. I'm sorry."

I tried to console her and told her to forget about what I said. I cared about her. But the setup was wrong. It was damaging on both sides. Even though I was warned against this kind of stuff by my parents, I didn't learn until I went through the motions myself. I was stubborn and immature. I had to see it for myself first. Even though Rima and I couldn't define our relationship over the phone, I was able to after a few days of reflection. I remember exactly where I was when it hit. It was about 4pm in the afternoon. I was sitting in my Introduction to Philosophy class. The topic of discussion was – suffering. Go figure.

"We are a vague ambiguous cloud of nothingness," I whispered to myself.

"Excuse me? What was that?" the Professor turned around and said searching for an inquisitive student with a question. Much to his disappointment, no one responded. I had to get out of there, I couldn't concentrate. I grabbed my books and walked out as soon as the Professor turned back around. Did he see me leave? I'm not sure. I had to get some air. I would end "things" with Rima, though she didn't take it well. But it was liberating. I felt like I could see clearer. I felt like I grew a little wiser after making that decision. It hurt, but you need to hurt to grow I suppose.

Later on that year I came across someone that taught me things without needing to say them. Her name was Layla. She was beautiful. Petite yet athletic. Olive skin and big green eyes. I couldn't tell you the color of her hair because I never saw it. She wore the *Hijab*. She wore it with such stunning modesty. She didn't look "foreign". She was like a Jasmine or a Pocahontas. Well aren't they foreign? Disney characters can't be foreign. They're American as American can be. It just flowed so nicely for her. The first time I saw her was walking out of lecture hall at the humanities building, as I waited for my class to start. She walked out as I walked in. Her eyes landed on mine, but she didn't smile. She didn't frown either. She struck me as a mixture of charming, professional, kind, and beautiful. I was determined to talk to her.

What I loved about Layla was that she actually rejected me. I introduced myself and asked about her class, since we were taking the same course but in different sections. She was lovely and outgoing, yet visibly reserved in her body language. Her nonverbal communication was on point. She didn't send mixed messages. She had this aura about her. It was special. When I tried to "talk" to her, she let me know politely, but firmly, that she didn't do *that*.

When it came to that area of life, things were black and white. There was no room to allow for grey areas. She didn't waste time. If you wanted to talk to her about anything other than school, work, and things of a professional nature then you were interested in something that she wasn't in the market for now. She was off limits. And once she was in the "market", you would have to court her through her family. I was annoyed at first, because I really did like her. But I respected her for letting me down. It was then that I realized that patience always bears good fruit. Even if I couldn't taste it then, it would wait for me. Layla wasn't the fruit, don't misunderstand. She was the agrarian who planted the seed.

That night at the shrine, I prayed for Rima and Layla. For Rima, I prayed that God would forgive us for hurting each other unnecessarily. For Layla, I prayed that God would protect her and give her someone that deserved her. I also prayed that the one who would deserve her would be me.

10. SUITS AND TURBANS

Our visit to Najaf actually coincided with an academic conference taking place at Kufa University. Professors from the United States, the United Kingdom, and Canada participated in the conference alongside professors from across the Middle East. Hadi and I didn't attend the conference, but we heard that its title was something along the lines of "Islam, Tolerance, and the Challenges of Modernity".

The Sayyid's son got a phone call from the organizers of the conference asking if the Sayyid would be amenable to a delegation of western professors visiting the Sayyid in his home. Being the prudent son and advisor that he was, he asked them for a list of names along with the academic institution they were affiliated with. One of those nights at Sayyid's home, his son came up to Hadi and I after getting off the phone.

"I did my research on these names and asked some contacts about them. They already passed security clearance. But I wanted to get your input and see if you may know something about these people that I didn't find out myself," he asked Hadi and I as he kneeled down to where we sat.

"Ali knows professors much more than I do," Hadi said as he grabbed the list and handed it to me.

I began reading the handwritten list and quickly came across a familiar name. Dr. Peter Stephens.

"This was my professor at my university. He taught Islamic History and Civilization." I pointed at the name as I looked up and said to the Sayyid's son.

"Was he open minded, friendly, shrewd? What do you know about him?" He asked as if trying to calculate all the possibilities of engagement and what expectations to have.

"He's shrewd. He is hard to read though. Some think he's an atheist, but I think that's a shallow reading of him. He's very sharp and intelligent. But he does seem to have some classical biases against Islam and its history."

"Ahsant. Thank you, Ali. I will let my father know. We may actually have them come here tonight. I want you to be here when they do." He looked so appreciative. He valued my input and acknowledged me. Again, I was humbled.

"Of course, it would be my honor."

He smiled and hurried out of the living room.

"Well done, Ali. Well done." Hadi gave me a soft clap until I clasped his hands and got him to stop. He was too much but never failed to crack me up.

Within an hour the meeting was confirmed and they were at the Sayyid's home within two. I realized the Sayyid was sensitive about who he met with and his office, managed by his son, was very meticulous when it came to the timing and arrangements of these meetings. That culture of precaution and prudence was something I came to learn was very prevalent amongst the scholars in the seminary. They felt a sense of responsibility for what they represented. They were intelligent in what they said and how they said it.

The visit started off with common pleasantries and welcoming of the guests. The guests reciprocated the welcome with their thanks and appreciation of being hosted by the Sayyid. I did notice that many of them didn't seem so comfortable sitting on the floor as we were. They weren't used to it. But they were trying. I chuckled to myself as I saw Professor Stephens try to find his element adjusting back and forth on the floor. Poor guy.

Taking it from a wider angle, the scene was breathtaking. You had a row of seven western professors, in their suits and sweater vests, sitting across from the Sayyid and a handful of his upper level students, all wearing turbans and the traditional garb of seminary scholars. In those moments, I couldn't categorize myself on either side. I was in dress pants and a button up. I had a small lightweight laptop to take notes of the discussions. I did this throughout the trip wherever possible, especially in gatherings with the scholars. I asked Hadi each time and he would tell me if it was appropriate or not. I had been in the company of scholars for days and it was enthralling. So when I looked at the scene again, between the seminarians and the academicians, I found myself literally in between suits and turbans.

Hadi sat next to the Sayyid to translate the questions to him. The Sayyid would answer and Hadi would translate back to the group. Live translation. I found it to be quite exciting. For one, I never saw Hadi, the goofball, in such a serious academic scenario. Two, I understood Arabic and could tell how well Hadi did in translating between the languages. Three, Hadi was sweating, I literally could see it on his forehead. I loved it!

The Sayyid's son did not fall short, even an inch, when it came to hospitality. Before Professor Stephens got too far in his search for a comfortable position on the floor, an arrangement of colorful tasty sweets, juice, and tea were graciously offered and gratefully accepted.

"I hope your stay in our beloved Iraq has been fruitful and inspiring thus far," the Sayyid said through Hadi.

The professors nodded with smiles as they chowed down on the plates of delicious *deheen* in front of them. Deheen is an Iraqi delicacy. So good and sweet and ever so sugary and fattening. But they ate it all up with no hint of remorse.

One of the professors from the United Kingdom introduced himself as the deheen was coming to an end. He was a rather distinguished chap. Young, tall, strong build, fair skin, salt and pepper beard, slick back hair with round glasses. He was a sharp looking guy.

"Respected Sayyid, my name is Anthony Greene. On behalf of us all, I'd like to thank you very much for welcoming us into your home. It is a distinct honor and privilege to be in your company," he said as he placed his hand on his heart. Sayyid smiled and nodded at the Professor as Hadi translated to him in Arabic.

"I had a question about Muslim thought on assimilation of Muslims in western societies. In England, and in other European countries for that matter, we have an ongoing challenge with Muslims actively choosing not to assimilate within greater society. Thus, they become isolated. In addition to having a plethora of preconceived notions of the Muslim faith and culture, Europeans fear the Muslims community because they do not know them. Is isolation in the West, a decree of the Islamic doctrine? What is the instructed method of engagement for Muslims in non-Muslim lands?"

This guy was impressive. I honestly didn't give these questions much thought before. I mean American Muslims are generally more assimilated than how the Professor was describing the situation in Europe, but I could relate to what he was saying nonetheless.

"Europe and the Americas are not the only places Islam was foreign to. Islam was foreign to Arabia in its early days of inception. And the same struggles of assimilation and isolation were faced during the Holy Prophet's era. Since then, there has been a middle path adopted by those wanting to follow in the Prophet's footsteps. That middle path is integration, but…"

"I am so sorry to interrupt you Honorable Sayyid. But you mentioned 'by those wanting to follow in the Prophet's footsteps', what do you mean by that? Again, my apologies," the British Professor said with his hands held together like a Christian prayer. I liked this guy. Intelligent and well mannered.

The Sayyid smiled and said, "Not a problem. Thank you for your question. These are the people who are genuinely dedicated to understanding their responsibilities through the Holy Quran and God's Prophet. They do not dismiss the Prophet's actions as inspired by anything other than revelation. In fact, they look at him as revelation itself. Not all Muslims practically do this, and this dates back to the days of the Prophet as well; hence, our emphasis on this.

"So, how do we see integration? What does it mean to us? Is it that you open a business with someone who is different than you in religion or race? Or that you invite people to your wedding that have different beliefs or customs? We as every other religion have our limitations that are meant to safeguard the integrity of our religious identity while we engage in society. For example, marriage is not permissible with someone who does not believe in God. Monotheism is a bare minimum. Marriage is a sacred institution and the starting point of a community. There are two essential principles for us. One, *alta'ayush* – coexistence. And two, *la ta'arrub ba'dil hijra...*"

Hadi struggled with that translation. He went back and forth with the Sayyid to clarify the meaning and make sure he was understanding the concept correctly. I admired his intent to be precise and accurate. I could tell he was taking this as a big responsibility and treating it seriously. It was a different side of Hadi. The delegation looked on in anticipation, waiting for the second principle that took additional time to translate and relay its meaning, and rightfully so. The expression was difficult and I couldn't think of a proper English translation either quite honestly.

Hadi finished up taking his notes as he listened intently to the Sayyid's clarifications and turned back to the group. He took a deep breath and said, "There is no 'Arabism' after migration. The term 'Arabism' is a reference to the nomadism of pre-Islamic times, or the Age of Ignorance. The principle here is that those who move to any land should not compromise his or her faith by going back to, or adopting, the habits and culture of his society if they are similarly contrary to the teachings of his or her faith."

Well done, Hadi! I almost jumped out of my seat and began clapping, but held it together before anyone caught wind of my inappropriate enthusiasm. Hadi did see me though as I squirmed in my seat with my ear-to-ear smile. He lowered his head down to his small notepad and pen to continue taking his vigorous notes as the Sayyid spoke. He covered his smile with his other hand.

The Sayyid continued. "We believe in integration. Not assimilation and not isolation. It is a path in between the two. We engage as everyone else in society should, while preserving our principles and our identity. Those who isolate themselves completely are wrong. And those who assimilate completely and lose their identity are wrong as well. We are not a religion of extreme approaches. We don't believe in extremism. It has never been a part of our prophetic culture and way of life." The Sayyid ended, again with a smile.

Professor Green smiled back and raised his prayer hands again towards the Sayyid. I noticed that all of the professors were taking notes on small notepads in their laps as the Sayyid was speaking, with the exception of one. Dr. Peter Stephens. The Sayyid's students on the other side of the room listened intently. They understood English, most if not all of them studied English as a second language at their universities. This group of Sayyid's students were longtime seminary students but had also studied at universities for their undergraduate studies, majoring in fields that ranged from chemical engineering to international affairs. They sat up straight in erect posture, holding masbahas in their hands that rested on their knees as they counted their prayer beads through small prayers.

Dr. Stephens was still struggling to find a comfortable position on the floor. Sayyid's son noticed that and asked him if he would like a chair.

"No, I'm fine thank you," he replied with a polite but half-hearted smile. Dr. Stephens was an older gentleman. Not so old, but older. Clean shaven and balding. He wore a bow-tie, all the time. A different bow-tie for each day though. It's like he had a collection of them. I remember counting the number of bow-ties he had one semester. I came up with seventeen. Seventeen! That's a lot of bow-ties for one guy.

Dr. Stephens turned towards the Sayyid and asked, "Sayyid, I have a question for you pertaining to religion. I teach history on the university level in the States. Frankly, I have found in my research over the years that religion is behind much of the problems we see in the world. Why does religion cause so much hate and bloodshed around the world? Sunnis and Shiites are at each other's throats. Protestants and Catholics killed one another for a hundred years. Muslims, Christians, and Jews continue to fight over Jerusalem, each claiming it is more rightfully theirs based on their religious superiority. So this isn't about Islam per se, but I guess it does take the lion's share of this reality particularly in modern times in the Middle East. So why do you think religion is such a problem?"

The question had the entire room chilled. Dr. Stephens came off arrogant and obnoxious. He was intelligent, but the question was more condescending and derogatory than intellectually stimulating. This was especially the case, given that he was visiting a religious scholar in his home. I was embarrassed for him.

Hadi whispered the translation to the Sayyid. The Sayyid nodded slowly as he listened to Hadi's reiteration while looking directly at the Professor. He didn't take his eyes off him. When Hadi was done, the Sayyid adjusted his posture, sat a bit taller, and smiled.

"Religion has surely caused all of the violence and hatred we witness in our world today. Better yet, it is responsible for the hatred, violence, and carnage caused across every age," the Sayyid paused and looked around the room.

"Do we truly believe this? Can we honestly say in our good conscience that religion is to blame for ails of the world? This is a narrative that is pushed by those of us who are not willing to continue our application of objectivity in every domain in which we observe and study. What happened to taking in all the variables affecting humanity for a sincere look at the challenges we face?" The Sayyid looked directly at Dr. Stephens.

"I want us to examine the history of man carefully. Give humanity, not religion, its due justice. Is it principle or whim that drives the conduct of man, when his pursuits are something other than benevolent? The misconduct we see in human beings is not a result of the practice of religion. It is the direct result of misusing the name of faith and an adulteration of its values to serve a personal pursuit. At the root of malice and capriciousness is not a religious belief, it is a deviation from intellect and an indulgence in desire, anger, or illusion. Corruption or bad behavior is not a result of religion, it's a result of the human condition."

"That is brilliant Respected Sayyid. I will include this in my next presentation at the university," Professor Greene added quickly as the Sayyid finished his answer. Dr. Stephens didn't seem completely satisfied. "Thank you for your hospitality once again, we do not wish to overstay our visit and impose especially since this was a last-minute arrangement." Professor Greene implicitly gestured for the other professors to get up. They lined up, shook the Sayyid's hands, and headed for the doors. The Sayyid's son waited at the door with a small gift for each of them.

Hadi announced to the group a message from Sayyid's son. "Before you leave, the Sayyid wished to give you a humble gift from the Holy City. These are precious stones that can be affixed on a ring or necklace if you would like. They are called Durr Najaf. Please accept our humble gift to you."

The professors were so happy. They beamed with smiles as they took their small stones and stored them away in their pockets for safe keeping. Some came up to me asking where they could get their stones affixed on rings. I didn't really know any shops. I tried to get Hadi's attention, but he was occupied translating for the Sayyid as one of the professors lingered to ask him a few questions privately. I asked the Sayyid's son and he provided some suggestions which I managed to translate.

I stopped Dr. Stephens on his way out. "Professor," I said. He turned around. "Yes?" He replied.

"You may not remember me, but I took your class a few years back at the University. It was Islamic History and Civilization."

"Ah, yes. I thought you looked familiar. What was your name again?"

"Ali."

"You must be a much more popular guy with that name here, huh?" he nudged me as he chuckled. What a weird thing to say.

"Yeah. Sure." I replied nonchalantly.

"It was good seeing you kid. Have fun here," he said as he walked outside through the door. Seriously? That's what you say to a student of yours that you see half way across the world? This guy was awful. Where are you in a hurry to go to? You're in Najaf. You don't have stuff going on right now. You came on a bus with the rest of the crew who were still inside!

But then I realized. The reason why he was acting like that was because he was embarrassed. He asked a challenging question, thinking that he was going to school the Sayyid through his subjectively objective rhetorical question. Instead, he got schooled. And Sayyid didn't even have to spend more than a minute or two in his response. At that point, I kind of just felt bad for the man. Poor guy.

I went up to the Sayyid afterwards and asked about the topic discussed earlier on integration. I wanted to understand it more. I couldn't wrap my head around the idea of integration. To me, it was you're either assimilated as an American, or you keep your distance so that you don't become Americanized. My mom spoke about integration but I couldn't see it. She and my dad were working most of the time and Emily was so immersed in her studies. They didn't have much time to really "engage" in society socially in a way that was outside their basic obligations for livelihood. And yeah, my sister's name was Emily, but so what? People still saw her as a Muslim hijabi girl. Did they accept her for who she was? Did they respect her? Did they understand her? She did a good job at holding her own and how she carried herself. But isn't there some sort of responsibility on the rest of society in regards to how they deal with us? And who assesses how much of that is to be weighed and valued here? I know I'm scattered. What else is new?

"Sayyid," I said. "Can I ask you a few questions about what you were telling Professor Greene?" We stood by the door as the last of the professors walked out of the house.

"Which topic was that?" the Sayyid asked as he scratched his beard.

"Integration," I said.

"Ah yes! Of course, ibni," he replied. Even though I could see he was clearly tired, he didn't turn me away. Instead, his eyes lit up and he smiled again. "Where would you like to start?"

"How should I look at this whole thing? I honestly don't know where to start," I replied as we sat back down on the floor.

"Ali keep this principle in mind. You are responsible for your actions and your actions alone. You deal with society on the basis of what you can control. What do you contribute to society? Look at that and focus on it. After that, we need to look at history and see how our community has dealt with these things as taught by the Imams over the years.

"Historically we have seen the integration of people in business and society. We do not need a specific decree to sanction integration. We have a general allowance in there being no problem with integration so long as it doesn't have a negative impact on you. This applies universally. It's derived from the principle of desiring a positive impact. We want there to be a higher likelihood that good comes from our engagement.

"The bare minimum for us in our principle of engagement is that we are not to be impacted negatively. Integrate and do not regress. The next is to impact positively. If you can, impact others positively and bring more good to your community through your integration. That is the optimal situation."

"But how do you do that? What do I do when I go back? Do I tell people about my religion? Do I make it a point to educate and explain stuff?" I asked him.

"Education is always a noble thing to be a part of. However, it is not necessary for us to be preachers. Nor is it a culture that the Imams promoted. They just wanted us to be ourselves and engage with people. Be who you claim to be. That is enough. People will see you for who you are."

The Sayyid went on to explain to me some deeper aspects of our history as Shia Muslims, and how we have witnessed a whole lot of persecution and suffering throughout the centuries. Much because of that the Shia had to be flexible, fluid, and adaptable.

"Your experience as a minority in the United States is unique; however, you and others in the West, generally, can learn from what we have witnessed historically as a Shia minority living within a Sunni majority society. It has consistently been part of the Shia narrative to be a minority. So that aspect is not foreign to us.

"Druze and Alawites experienced much of the same persecution as Twelver Shias. They chose a different path though. They chose to be isolated. Because of their isolation they became *madhaheb batiniya* – esoteric sects. Secretive, enigmatic, and even misconstrued. A lot of that was a direct effect of their choice to be isolated in the context of persecution and the climate they lived in."

"So you're saying the Shia didn't isolate? They always integrated?" I asked.

"That is what our Imams guided us to do. Did we always implement? Not necessarily. Over the span of centuries was our trend to do so? Yes. Humans will generally have their progress and their moments of regression. But they cannot be crippled by fear. Integration comes when you don't have fear. Isolation is a direct re-sult of fear."

If I am strong enough to engage, I should dive in with no fear. But if I am weak, I am probably scared. If I'm scared, I'll probably just stick to myself. I needed to work on my strength. I was tired of being weak and suc-cumbing to my whimsical desires. Most of all, I was tired of being afraid. I no longer wanted to be shackled by my uncertainty in my own identity. I could no longer tolerate my inaction and lack of faith. Why did I continue to question myself when the truth was so evident? I had everything I needed. All the tools were at my disposable. All I needed to do was look within. It was there that I would find the greater universe.

11. ICE CREAM IN NAJAF

"So what boggles your mind? What itches your skin?" The Sayyid asked me as we walked up to the colorful ice cream parlor on Al-Rasool Street.

I looked at him confused. It probably seemed like half of this trip I was confused, if not more than half.

"I'm not talking about mosquitos. I'm talking about that one question that keeps you up at night. What is it?" He continued.

Staring at the pictures of ice cream flavors above the small counter in the street store I said, "I don't know. I don't think I have one of those."

"One pomegranate ice cream cup please," the Sayyid told the young man behind the counter. Within seconds the young man had the ice cream ready and handed it to the Sayyid.

"Here you go son," the Sayyid said as he gave me the cup of ice cream.

"What about you Sayyid? Aren't you going to eat?"

"Too much sugar for me. You enjoy," he smiled.

I took a bite out of the pomegranate flavored delight and was suddenly inspired. "But I do ask myself at times what am I here for? What is my purpose? I mean what really is my purpose? What makes me different than the next person? I feel like I know what my purpose should be... but what is it really? Am I who I think I am?" I then paused as the dawning question after those series of questions crashed down on me. I whispered looking away, "I mean... who am I?"

The Sayyid smirked and said, "I take it you like *Rumman*." That's what it was called in Arabic. I loved Rumman.

Not sure if it was the flavor or the sugar. Or both. But I had a mixture of excitement and nervousness about me. Still, it was some good ice cream. Probably the best I ever had.

"Well, you're not the first to ask the existential question nor will you be the last. It's part of life, and there is no set time or phase in which one asks these questions looking for deeper meaning in life. These sort of questions often come during young adulthood. But then again how old is a 'young adult'? I feel like I'm a young adult and I'm 55. How's that for identity and purpose?"

That made me chuckle and I was eased by the Sayyid's humor. It was amazing to see an individual of his stature and prestige be able to be so down to earth and humorous. It provided me with a sense of security, one that I could only compare to that of my father.

"Your purpose is what you make it. There's no set way to go about it or defined details that it must include. The clearer it is to you, the better. Because then it will better guide you. You can have a framework, one that applies universally to all of us. That framework is simple. We are here to be the best possible versions of ourselves, striving for excellence. You need at least that. Then you need to deepen it. That comes with maturity and growth. Your purpose deepens over time. Some of us take longer than others. Some know it so clearly so early on. But even if we don't have depth, we at least need some shallow water. Otherwise, we'd be completely dry and nothing can live when it's dying of thirst."

That fascinated me. But then he hit another cord within me that I never knew someone could articulate for me.

"How can someone so able feel fulfilled and so empty at the same time. Contentment is fleeting, and emptiness can be consuming. It's as if nothing mattered because there's a hole that never seems to fill. When will it ever be filled? What must be done? What must change? The world's a stage and you're its greatest actor. You love the stage, but you grow tired of it. It's a job you're so good at but just don't feel like... like it's you. Or the you that you want.

"This is often the suffering of those of us with privilege. Privilege is both a great blessing and a curse. It allows us to help those that need help, but it also blinds us to the reality of what it's like to actually be in need. We are in need of so many things in that privilege. We are in need of sight. Because we are blind to our selfishness. We are in need of warmth. Because we have become cold to others. We are in need of guidance. Because we are lost to our whims. We are in need of purpose. Because we do not know who we are."

"Have you ever felt helpless?"

"Sure, I have."

"What made you feel helpless?"

I thought back to my recent incident of being stranded in Hines Park. I remembered how lost I felt and what caving into the sins of my flesh got me to. Helpless? I felt more than helpless. I felt insignificant, unworthy of mentioning.

"Why do you want details?" I replied sharply at the Sayyid. I quickly realized my tone changed and regretted it deeply. I feared that I disrespected him. He didn't judge or change his speech.

He replied, "Details are nothing more than being more definitive to communicate ideas more effectively. I don't ask for entertainment. I ask for clarity."

I didn't answer. I was still embarrassed by the way I shot back. He continued.

"You feel helpless when you fall to sin. When you fall to the same impulsive desires. It may be your hunger for food, attention, sex, influence, or even just the desire to indulge in doing nothing at all. In those moments, when you know you have given up control of yourself, when you gave away your decision-making to someone or something else... that is when you feel helpless."

It was as if he read my thoughts that traveled back to the park when I woke up not knowing where I was, trying to hold myself from having a panic attack.

"How did you..."

"That's when we all feel helpless, Ali."

"So, what is your purpose?" I covered my mouth as if the words slipped out and I was trying to bring them back to where they sprouted. I wasn't successful.

"My purpose..." The Sayyid sighed and looked on. "My purpose is to be free. To be free of the shackles of everything in the way of being fully present and aware. To lead myself truly and not be led."

"To lead yourself within the system or to break free from it completely?" I asked.

"You can't break free from the system. Instead you must master it. Integrate within it, be a part of it, but then masterfully own it. It's a mistake to think one can completely break free from it. That's not freedom. That's isolation and aversion."

"Sayyid I don't mean to transgress but..."

"Don't hesitate son, ask."

"Is your answer provided through your lens as an Islamic scholar, an Iraqi, an Arab or what? What lens are you looking through?"

"In the end what's a lens to tell you beyond experiences associated with some parts of your identity. Scholar. Student. Iraqi. American. Privileged. Poor. Integrated. Isolated. Parts and pieces. What is the root? What is really there? Beneath all of that? A human being. Created to be amazing. But dragged down by the mud of life and the challenges it brings.

"What makes us human beings, what makes us mankind is our ability to see a challenge, to face the adversity, and overcome it. It is our choice, our decision, our free will that allows us to transcend beyond the rest of God's creation. What does it mean to be human? What does it mean to be a man? And what does it mean to be truly alive in our sense of life? It is that. To choose to be as you wish to be. Not as your whims wish to be or your impulsive passions move you to be, but rather as your destined self of greatness ought to be."

"I want that to be my purpose," I said hopefully.

"Your purpose should be your own. You have a framework. But make it your own. Don't take on a purpose because it sounds nice off the tongue of another. It needs to come from within. If not, it won't be sincere. Without sincerity, you will not have the commitment you need because there is no real conviction in your heart of your purpose. It must be you."

He spoke to my heart. All the answers he gave, I understood and felt. Questions I had were being answered and even questions I haven't asked before were coming to light with understanding. He gave me depth. I had had a foundation. I had a framework. He expanded it for me. I was ever so grateful.

We finished our ice cream and headed back to our building. It was my last day in Najaf. My flight back was in a few hours and I still needed to pack. I wanted to spend the last bit of time I had with the Sayyid. He gave me so much that I just wanted more. It was like salt water with him. No matter how much I drank, I couldn't get enough to quench my thirst. But in the end, I would be forced to take my last sips even if I was not quenched.

I gave my farewells to the Sayyid and embraced him so tight. I cried on his shoulder. I tried to conceal it but he felt it nonetheless. He rubbed my back and whispered a prayer in my ear.

Call onto Ali, the Revealer of Miracles

You will find him in your times of need

Every worry and woe will be removed

By your guard O' Ali, O' Ali, O' Ali

That whispered prayer continued to echo in my ear. Though I only heard it once from the Sayyid, I memorized it and repeat it every day now before I go to bed. It brings me a calmness I never thought I could have. There are things that are not in our control. Some things are gifted to us by God's grace and we are merely blessed with their benefits and bounties. I think this was one of them for me.

When I came back home, I couldn't tell you that I came back a new man. I couldn't tell you that I said goodbye to my old self. I couldn't tell you I was forever changed. That may be the case with other people. They come back from an experience like Ziyara, Hajj, or something else that was spiritually uplifting and speak of their aha-moment. They found their moment of self-discovery or actualization and held on to it for dear life. I didn't have a moment like that. And I'm not so sure that is what I was or should have been looking for anyway.

Maybe if I looked for that type of a moment, I would have been disappointed by the lack of it. But I was content. I lived the enlightening experience and soaked it in as much as I could without tainting it with expectations. Maybe it was a defense-mechanism, to keep me from feeling disappointed. Maybe it was a blessing in disguise, to realize that what really mattered was how the experience would prove to change me for the better and not how "aha-moment" the experience was. Maybe it was both.

What I did have was an indescribable experience that tapped into so many dimensions of my life. Najaf gave me greater depth into my own self and helped me transcend the lack of clarity I struggled with. There was smoke in my eyes and what was foggy before was now becoming clear. I not only deepened my connection to my faith spiritually and intellectually, I was blessed to do so in such a personal way. From the very meaning and purpose of my name to the family and lineage I belonged to, I gained a greater sense of self. I realized that that sins and shortcomings of my past were not mere transgressions of desire, they were a product of confusion in identity.

My journey didn't save my soul. I wasn't lost to be found. I wasn't sick to be cured. I wasn't dead to be brought to life. But there definitely was smoke and during my journey I began to clear it. Hadi, the Sayyid, and Najaf altogether, helped me see through the smoke. They helped me see my true spirit, who I really was and who I could be. It was a good spirit, a beautiful one in fact. It was one that was formed by my Lord and cared for by Mama, Baba, Emily, and Adam. But in the end it was my responsibility. I had the choice to clear the smoke, no matter how often it came back and blurred my vision. It was always my choice.

Upon my return, I chose to walk the shores of Lake Michigan again and not only dip my feet in the water but dive in for a swim. Surely, the Great Lakes of Michigan are a great reminder for me, that I'll always be a fish of the Mediterranean Sea. I knew who I was. I knew what I came from. I knew where I was going.

I finally chose to see.

"Ali, what are you looking at?" I heard Emily's voice from behind me as I stared out the window of Mama's hospital room. I was still swimming. In my lakes of thoughts and the sea of life, I was swimming and it felt great. I embraced it.

I turned around and smiled. Emily smiled back, as she always did. I didn't need to say anything. She understood when she saw my smile. She saw that I was looking within. That I saw the greater universe... that I finally saw *me*.

ABOUT THE AUTHOR

Growing up in his father's pizzerias, both in Dearborn, MI and Tyre, Lebanon, Jalal Moughania developed a strong work ethic, confidence in his identity, and an unwavering love for pizza and calzones. He is now a practicing attorney, author, and public speaker. Moughania has written, translated, and edited over ten books. He currently resides with his wife and daughter in Dearborn Heights, MI.

Made in the USA
San Bernardino, CA
03 January 2019